I0649378

Mayne Reid

**The Free Lances**

Vol. 1

Mayne Reid

**The Free Lances**
*Vol. 1*

ISBN/EAN: 9783337347321

Printed in Europe, USA, Canada, Australia, Japan

Cover: Foto ©Andreas Hilbeck / pixelio.de

More available books at **www.hansebooks.com**

# THE FREE LANCES.

## A ROMANCE OF THE MEXICAN VALLEY.

BY

## CAPTAIN MAYNE REID.

IN THREE VOLUMES.

## VOL. III.

LONDON:

REMINGTON & CO.,

134 NEW BOND STREET,

1881.

# CONTENTS.

# THE FREE LANCES.

## Chapter XLIII.

### WHAT ARE THEY?

HE repast finished, the Holy Brethren, rising from the table together, forsook the Refectory. Some disappeared into cloisters on the sides of the great hallway, others strolled out in front, and seating themselves on benches that were about, commenced rolling and smoking cigarittos.

The Abbot excusing himself to his stranger guests, on plea of pressing business, was invisible for a time. So they were permitted to betake themselves apart. Good manners secured them this. The others naturally supposed they might want a word in private, so no one offered to intrude upon them.

Just what they did want, and had been anxiously longing for. They had mutually to communicate ; questions to be asked, and counsel taken together. Each was burning to know what the other thought of the company they had fallen into ; the character of which was alike perplexing to both.

After getting hold of their hats they sauntered out by the great door, through which they had entered on the night before. The sun was now at meridian height, and his beams fell down upon the patch of open ground in front of the monastery ; for a monastery they supposed it must be. A glance backward as they walked out from its walls showed its architecture purely of the conventual style ; windows with pointed arches, the larger ones heavy mullioned, and a campanile upon the roof. This however, without bells, and partially broken down ; as was much of the outer mason work everywhere. Here and there were walls crumbling to decay, others half hidden under masses of creeping plants and cryptogams, in short the whole structure seemed more or less dilapidated.

Soon they entered under the shadow of the trees ; long-leaved evergreen pines loaded with parasites and epiphytes, among these several species of orchids—rare phenomenon in the vegetable world, that would have delighted the eye of a botanist. As they wished to get beyond earshot of those left lounging by the porch, they continued on along a walk which had once been gravelled, but was now overgrown with weeds and grass. It formed a cool arcade, the thick foliage meeting over-head, and screening it from the rays of the sun. Following it for about a hundred yards or so, they again had the clear sky before them, and saw they were on the brow of a steep slope—almost a precipice—which, after trending a short distance right and left, took a turn back toward the mass of the mountain. It was the boundary of the platform on which the building stood with a still higher cliff behind.

The point they had arrived at was a prominent one, affording view of the whole valley of Mexico, that lay spread out like a picture at their feet. And such a picture! Nothing in all the panoramic world to excel —if equal it.

But as scenery was not in their thoughts they gave it but a glance, sitting down with faces turned towards one another. For there were seats here also—several rustic chairs under shady trees—it being evidently a favourite loitering place of the friars.

"Well, Cris, old comrade," said Kearney first to speak, "we've gone through a good deal this day or two in the way of change. What do you think of these new acquaintances of ours ? "

"Thar, Cap., ye put a puzzler."

"Are they monks ? "

"Wal ; them is a sort o' anymals I haint had much dealin's wi' ; niver seed any till we kim inter Mexiko, 'ceptin' one or two as still hangs round San Antone in Texas. But this chile knows little u' thar ways, only from what he's heerin ; an' judging be that he'd say thar ain't nerry monk among 'em."

"What then? Robbers?"

"Thar, agin, Cap., I'm clean confuscated. From what we war told o' Mr. Reevus in the gaol, they oughter be that. They sayed he war a captain o' *saltadores*, which means highwayman. An' yet it do 'pear kewrous should be sich."

"From what I know of him," rejoined Kearney, " what I learned yesterday, it would be curious indeed—remarkably so. I've reason to believe him a gentleman born, and that his title of captain comes from his having been an officer in the army."

" That mou't be an' still wouldn't contrary his havin' turned to t'other. Down by the the Rio Grande, thar are scores o' Mexikin officers, who've did the same, from lootenants, up to kurnels—aye ginrals. Thar's Canales, who commanded the whole cavalry brigade— the " Chaperal fox " as we Texans call him—

an' thar ain't a wuss thief or cut-throat from Matamoras up to the mountains. An' what air ole Santy hisself but a robber o' the meanest an' most dastardly sort? So, taint any sign o' honesty their bearing military titles. When they've a war on in thar revolushionary way, they turn sogers, atween times takin' to the road."

"Well, Cris, supposing these to be on the road now, what ought we to do, think you?"

"Neery use thinkin', Cap.; since thar's no choice left us. Taint die dog, or ect the hatchet; and this chile goes for chawin the steel. Whativer they be, we're bound to stick to 'em, an' oughter be glad o' the chance, seein' we haint the shadder o' another. If tuk agin' we'd be strung up or shot sure. Highwaymen or lowwaymen, they're the only ones about these diggins that kin gie us

purtekshun, an' I reck'n, we may rely on them
for that—so far's they're able."

For a time Kearney was silent, though not
thinking over what the Texan had said;
much of which had passed through his mind
before. The train of his reflections were
carried further back; to the point where he
was first brought into contact with Rivas,
by their legs getting linked together. Then
forward throughout the hours and incidents
that came after; recalling everything that
had occurred, in act as in conversation—
mentally reviewing all, in an endeavour to
solve the problem that was puzzling them.

Seeing him so occupied, and with a suspicion of how his thoughts were working, the
Texan forebore further speech, and awaited
the result.

"If we've fallen among banditti," Kearney
at length said, "it will be awkward to get away

from them. They'll want us to take a hand
at their trade, and that wouldn't be nice."

"Sartinly not, Cap.; anything but agreeable
to eyther o' us. It goes agin the grit o' a
honest man to think o' belonging to a band o'
robbers. But forced to jine 'em that 'ud be
different. Besides, the thing ain't the same in
Mexico, as 'twud in Texas and the States.
Hyar 'tisn't looked on as beein' so much o' a
disgrace, s'long's they don't practize cruelty.
An' I've heern Mexikins say, 'taint wuss, nor
yet so bad, as the way some our oun poltishun
an' lawyers plunder the people. I guess it be
'bout the same, when one gits used to it."

To this quaint rigmarole of reasoning—not
without reason in it, however—Kearney only
replied with a smile, allowing the Texan to
to continue ; which he did saying :

"After all, I don't think they're robbers
any more than monks ; if they be, they're

wonderfully well-behaved. A perliter set o'
fellers or better kump'ny this chile niver war
in durin the hull coorse of his experience in
Texas, or otherwhars. They ain't like to lead
us into anythin' very bad, in the way o'
cruelty or killin'. So I say, let's freeze to e'm,
till we find they ain't worthy of being froze
to ; then we must gie 'em the slip, somehow."

"Ah ! if we can," said his fellow filibuster
doubtingly. "But that is the thing for the
far hereafter. The question is what are we to
do now ?"

"No guess'n at all, Cap., as thar's no
choosin' atween. We're boun' to be robbers
for a time, or whatsomever else these new
'quaintances 'o ours be themselves. Thet's
sure as shootin'."

"True," returned the other, musingly.
"There seems no help for it. It's our fate,
old comrade ; though one, I trust, we shall be

able to control without turning highwaymen.
I don't think they are that. I can't believe
it."

"Nor me neyther. One thing, howsomever,
thet I hev obsarved air a leetle queery, an'
sort o' in thar favour."

"What thing ?"

"Thar not hevin' any weemen among 'em.
I war in the kitchen this mornin' 'fore ye war
up, and kedn't see sign o' a petticoat about ;
the cookin' bein' all done by men sarvents.
Thet, I've heern say, air the way wi' monks ;
but not wi' the other sort. What do you
make o't, Cap.?"

"I hardly know, Cris. Possibly the Mexican brigands, unlike those of Italy, don't care
to encumber themselves with a following of
the fair sex."

"On t'other hand," pursued the Texan, "it
seems to contrary their bein' o' the religious

sort, puttin' out sentries as they do. Thar
wor that one we passed last night and this
mornin' I seed two go out wi' guns, one takin'
each side, and soon arter two others comin' in
as if they'd been jest relieved from thar posts.
Thar's a path as leads down from both sides o'
the building."

"All very strange, indeed," said Kearney.
"But no doubt ws shall soon get explanation
of it. By the way," he added, changing tone
with the subject, "where is the dwarf? What
have they done with him?"

"That I can't tell eyther, Cap. I havn't
seen stime o' the critter since he war tuk away
from us by that head man o' the sarvents, and
I don't wish ever to set eyes on the skunk
again. Cris Rock niver was so tired o' a
connexshun as wi' thet same. Wagh!"

"I suppose they've got him shut up somewhere, and intend so keeping him—no doubt

for good reasons. Ah ! now we're likely to hear something about the disposal of ourselves. Yonder comes the man who can tell us !"

This, as the *soi-disant* Abbot was seen approaching along the path.

## Chapter XLIV.

## THE ABBOT.

" *MIGO*," said their host, as he rejoined them, speaking to Kearney who could alone understand him, " Permit me to offer you a cigar—your comrade also—with my apologies for having forgotten that you smoked. Here are both Havannas and Manillas, several brands of each. So choose for yourself."

The mayor-domo, who attended him, carrying a huge mahogany case had already placed it upon one of the rustic benches, and laid open the lid.

" Thanks, holy father," responded Kearney with a peculiar smile. " If you have no objection, I'll stick to the Imperadoes. After smoking one of them a man need have no difficulty as to choice."

At which he took an " Emperor " out of the case.

" I'm glad you like them," observed the generous donor helping him to a light. " They ought to be of good quality considering what they cost and where they come from. But, Don Florencio, don't let the question of expense hinder you smoking as many as you please. My outlay on them was *nil;* they were a contribution to the monastery ; though not exactly a charitable one."

He said this with a sort of inward laugh, as

though some strange history attached to the Imperadoes.

" A forced contribution, then," thought the Irishman, the remark having made a strange, and by no means pleasant impression upon him.

The Texan had not yet touched the cigars, and when with a gesture the invitation was extended to him, he hung back, muttering to Kearney :

" Tell him, Cap., I'd purfar a pipe ef he ked accomerdate me wi' thet ere article."

" What says the Señor Cristoforo ?" asked the Abbot.

" He'd prefer smoking a pipe, if you don't object, and there be such a thing convenient."

" Oh ! *un pipa.* I shall see. Gregorio !"

He called after the mayor-domo, who was returning toward the house.

" Never mind, reverend Father," protested

Kearney, " Content yourself with a cigar, Cris, and don't give trouble."

I'm sorry I spoke o' it," said the Texan. " I oughter be only too gled to git a seegar, an' it may be he wudn't mind my chawin', stead o' smoking' it ! My stammuck feels starved for a bit o' bacca. What wouldn't I gie jest now for a plug o' Jeemes's River !"

" There, take one of the cigars and eat it if you like, I'm sure he'll have no objection."

Availing himself of the leave thus vicariously accorded, the Texan picked out one of the largest in the collection and, biting off about a third, commenced crunching it between his teeth, as though it was a piece of sugar-stick. This to the no small amusement of the Mexican, who, however, delicately refrained from making remark.

Nor was Cris hindered from having a smoke as well as a " chew,"—The mayor-domo soon after appearing with a pipe, a somewhat eccentric affair he had fished out from the back regions of the establishment.

Meanwhile their host had himself lit one of the " Emperors," and was smoking away like a chimney. A somewhat comical sight at any time, or in any place, is a monk with a cigar in his mouth. But that the Abbot of the Serro Ajusco was no anchorite they were already aware, and saw nothing in it to surprise them.

Seating himself beside Kearney, with face turned towards the valley, he put the question :—

" What do you think of that landscape, Don Florencio ?"

" Magnificent ! I can't recall having looked upon lovlier, or one with greater variety of scenic detail. It has all the elements of the sublime and beautiful."

The young Irishman was back in his college classics with his countryman Burke.

" Make use of this," said the Abbot, offering a small telescope which he drew out. " 'Twill give you a better view of things."

Taking the glass and adjusting it to his sight, Kearney commenced making survey of the valley, now bringing one portion of it within the field of telescopic vision, then another.

" Can you see the Pedregal?" asked the Abbot. " It's close in to the mountain's foot. You'll recognise it by its sombre grey colour."

" Certainly I see it," answered the other, after depressing the telescope. " And the thicket we came through on its further side— quite distinctly."

" Look to the right of that, then you'll observe a large house, standing in the middle

of the magüey fields. Have you caught
it ?"

" Yes ; why do you ask ?"

" Because that house has an interest for me
—a very special one. Whom do you suppose
it belongs to ; or I should rather say, did and
ought to belong to ?"

" How should I know, holy Father ?" asked
Kearney thinking it somewhat strange his
being so interrogated.

" True," responded the Abbot, " how could
you, my son. But I'll tell you. That
*magueyal* is mine by right ; though by wrong
'tis now the property of our late host, the
Governor of the Acordada. His reward at the
last confiscation for basely betraying his
country and our cause."

" What cause ?" inquired the young Irishman, laying aside the glass, and showing more
interest in what he heard than that he had

been looking at. Country and cause! These were not the words likely to be on the lips of either monk or highwayman.

And that the man who had spoken to him was neither one nor other he had fuller proof in what was now further said :—

" A cause, Señor Irlandes, for which I, Ruperto Rivas, am ready to lay down life, if the sacrifice be called for, and so most—I may say all—of those you've just met at *almuerzo*. You heard it proclaimed in the toast " Patria y Libertad !"

" Yes. And a grand noble sentiment it is. One I was gratified to hear."

" And surprised as well. Is not that so, *amigo ?*"

" Well, to be frank with you, holy Father, I confess to something of the sort."

" Not strange you should, my son. No doubt you're greatly perplexed at what you've seen and heard since you came up here, with much before. But the time has come to relieve you. So light another cigar and listen."

## Chapter XLV.

### THE FREE LANCES.

"RY a Manilla this time," said the Mexican, as Kearney was reaching out to take a cigar from the case. "Most people believe that the best can only come from Cuba. A mistake that. There are some made in the Phillippine Islands equal —in my opinion, superior—to any Havannahs. I speak of a very choice article, which don't ever get into the hands of the dealers, and's

only known to the initiated. Some of our
*ricos* import them by way of Acapulco.
Those are a fair sample."

The young Irishman made trial of the weed
thus warmly recommended ; to discover what
contradicted all his preconceived ideas in the
smoking line. He had always heard it said
that the choicest cigars are Havannahs ; but,
after a few whiffs from that Manilla, which
had never seen a cigar shop, he was willing to
give up the " Imperadores ".

His host lighting one of the same, thus
proceeded :

" *Pues, caballero ;* to give you the promised
explanation. That the monks of my com-
munity are of an order neither very devout or
austere, you've already observed no doubt,
and may have a suspicion they're not monks
at all. Soldiers every man ; most having seen
service, and many who have done gallant

deeds. When I speak of them as soldiers, you will understand it in its true sense, Señor. With one or two exceptions all have held commissions in our army, and with a like limitation, I may say are all gentlemen. The last revolution, which has again cursed our country by restoring its chronic tyrant, Santa Anna, of course threw them out ; the majority, as myself, being proscribed, with a price set upon their heads."

" Then you're not robbers ?"

This was said without thought, the words involuntarily escaping Kearney's lips. But the counterfeit abbot, so far from feeling offence at them, broke out into a laugh, good-humouredly rejoining—

" Robbers, *amigo mio !* Who told you we were that ?"

The Irishman felt abashed, seeing he had committed himself.

"Don Ruperto," he exclaimed, hastening to make the best of his blunder, "I owe you every apology. It arose from some talk I heard passing around in the prison. Be assured, I neither did nor could believe it."

"Thank you, Señor!" returned the Mexican. "Your apologies are appreciated. And," he added, putting on a peculiar smile, "in a way superfluous. I believe we do enjoy that repute among our enemies ; and to confess the truth, not without some reason."

Kearney pricked up his ears, perplexity, with just a shade of trouble, again appearing upon his face. He said nothing, however, allowing the other to proceed.

"*Carramba*, yes!" continued the proscript. "'Tis quite true we do a little in the plundering line—now and then. We need doing it, Don Florencio. But for that I mightn't have been able to set so good a breakfast before you ; nor wines of such quality, nor yet these delectable cigars. If you look to the right down there, you'll see the *pueblo* of San Augustin, and just outside its suburbs a large yellow house. From that came our last supply of drinkable and smokable materials, including those here, mahogany and every-thing. A forced contribution, as I've hinted at. But, señor, I should be sorry to have you think we levy black-mail indiscriminately. He from whom they were taken is one of our bitterest enemies ; equally an enemy of our country. 'Twas all in the way of reprisal ; fair, as you'll admit, when you come to com-prehend the circumstances."

" I comprehend them now," returned the listener, relieved, " quite ; and I trust you will accept my apology."

" *Sans arriere pensee*," responded the Mexi-can, who could speak French if not English,

"I do frankly, freely. No reproach to you for supposing us robbers. I believe many others do, among whom we make appearance. Southward, however, in the State of Oaxaca, we are better known as 'the Free Lances'. A title not so appropriate either, since our weapons are only at the disposal of the Republic—our lives as well."

"But," questioned Kearney, "may I ask why you are habited as I now see you?"

"For a good reason, *amigo*. It adds to our security, giving all sorts of opportunities. Throughout Mexico, the cowl of the monk is the best passport a man could be provided with. Wearing it we go about among the mountain villages without suspicion, the people believing that this old monastery, so long abandoned as to have been forgotten, has again become the dwelling place of a religous order. Of course, we don't allow any of the rustics to approach it. Luckily they are not curious enough to care for that, against the toil of climbing up here. If they attempt it we have sentinels to stay them. For ourselves we have learned to play the part of the holy friar, so that there would be difficulty in detecting the counterfeit. As it chances we have with us one or two who once wore the cowl. These perverts have taught us all the tricks and passwords current among the fraternity. Hitherto they have availed us, and I trust will, till the time arrives for our casting off our cassock and putting on the soldier's coat. That day is not distant, Don Florencio ; nearer than I expected, from what my comrades have told me since we came up. The State of Oaxaca is disaffected; as indeed the whole southern side of Acapulco, and a *grito* is anticipated ere long—possibly within a month. Alvarez, who controls in that quarter, will be

the man to raise it ; and the old Pinto chief
will expect to be joined by the ' Free Lances '.
Nor will he be disappointed. We are all
burning to be at it. So, caballero, you see
how it is with us. And now," he added,
changing tone and looking his listener earnestly in the face, " I have a question to put
to yourself."

" What ?" asked the Irishman, seeing that
he hesitated puting it.

" Will you be one of us ?"

It was now Kearney's turn to hesitate about
the answer he ought to make. A proposition
fraught with such consequences required consideration. To what would he be committing
himself if he consented ? And what if he
should refuse ? Besides under the circumstances was he free to refuse ? That of itself
was a question, a delicate one. He and his
comrade Cris Rock owed their escape to this

strange man, whatever he might be : and to separate from him now, even under full permission, would savour of ingratitude. Still more after listening to what was further said. For noting his embarrassment, and deeming it natural enough the Mexican hastened to relieve him.

"If my proposal be not to your liking, Señor Irlandes, say so; and without fear of offence. All the same, you may rest assured of our protection while you remain with us; and I shall do what I can to get you safe out of the country. At all events, I won't send you back to the Accordada goal and the tender care of its governor. So you can speak frankly without reserve. Are you willing to be one of us?"

"I am!" was the answer given without further hesitation.

Why should he have either hesitated or

said nay ? In the heart of a hostile country, an escaped prisoner; his life, as he felt sure, forfeited should he be retaken. Joining Rivas and his Free Lances might be his sole chance of saving it. Even had they been banditti he could not have done better then.

" Yes, Don Ruperto," he added, "if you deem me worthy of belonging to your brotherhood, be it so. I accept your invitation."

"And your comrade, Don Christoforo. Will he be of the same mind, think you ? "

" Sure to be. I take it, I can answer for him. But you shall hear for yourself. Rock ! "

He called to the Texan, who, not understanding their dialogue, had sauntered apart, chewing away at the Imperador.

" Wal, Cap.; what's up now ? " he asked on rejoining them.

"They're no robbers. Cris," said Kearney, speaking freely in their own tongue.

"Gled to hear it, I did'nt think they war— noways. Nor monks neyther, I guess?"

"Nor monks."

"What then, Cap.?"

"The same as yourself. Patriots who have been fighting for their country, and got defeated. That's why they are here— in hiding."

"Yis, Cap.; I see it all, clar as coon's track on a mud bar. Enemies o' ole Santy, who've got beat it thar last risin'."

"Just so. But they expect another rising soon, and wish us to join them. I've agreed and said so. What say you?"

"Lordy, Cap.: what a questun to be axed, an by yurself! Sure this chile air boun to stick to ye, whatsomever ye do. Ef they'd been brigants I shed a put my conscience

in my pocket, an goe'd in wi'em all the same ;
s'long you're agreed. Nor I wud'nt a
minded turning monk for a spell. But men
who intend foughtin for freedom ? Haleluyah !
Cris Rock air all thar ! Ye may tell him
so."

"He consents," said Kearney, reporting
to the Mexican ; "and willingly as myself.
Indeed, Don Ruperto, we ought both to
regard it as a grace—an honour—to be so
associated, and we shall do the best we can
to show ourselves worthy of it."

"*Mil gracioas, Señor!* The grace and
honour are all given to us. Two such
*valientes*, as I know you to be, will be no
slight acquisition to our strength. And
now, may I ask you to assume the garb
which as you see is our present uniform ?
That by way of precaution for the time.
You'll find suitable raiment inside. I've

given Gregorio orders to get it ready. So you see, *Camarados,* I've been counting upon you."

"Gehosofat!" exclaimed the Texan, when told of the dress he was expected to put on. "What wi New-Orleen's store close, an' prison duds, an' the like, this chile hev hed a goodish wheen o' changes since he stripped off his ole huntin' shirt. An' now a goin· in for a monk! Wal; tho' I mayen't be the most santified, I reck'n I'll be the tallest in thar mon'stery."

# Chapter XLVI.

## ST. AUGUSTINE OF THE CAVES.

NE of the pleasantest villages in the valley of Mexico is San Augustin de las Cuevas—*Tlalpam* by Aztec designation — both names due to some remarkable caverns in the immediate neighbourhood. It is some ten or twelve miles from the capital, on the southern or Acapulco road, just where this, forsaking the valley level begins to ascend the Sierra, passing over which by Cruz del Marques, it continues on through the *tierras calentes* of Cuernavaca and Guerrero to the famed port of the Pacific.

San Augustin is a *pueblo*, endowed with certain municipal privileges. It boasts of an *alcalde-mayor* with other corporate officers, and a staff of alguezils, or policemen.

The heads of departments are mostly men of pure Spanish race—" gente de razon," as they proudly proclaim themselves—though many are in reality of mixed blood, Mestizos. Of this are the better class of shopkeepers, few in number, the *gente de razon* at best forming a scarce discernible element in the population, which is mainly made up of the brown aborigines.

At a certain season of the year, however, paler complexions show in the ascendant. This during carnival time—"*Las Pascuas*".

Then the streets of San Augustin are crowded with gay promenaders; while carriages and men on horseback may be seen in continuous stream passing to and fro between it and the capital. In Las Pascuas week, one day with another, half Mexico is there engaged in a gambling orgie, as Londoners at Epsom during the Derby. More like Homburg and Monaco, though; since the betting at Tlalpam is not upon the swiftness of horses, but done with dice and cards. The national game, "monte," there finds fullest illustration, grand marquees being erected for its play—real temples erected to the goddess Fortuna. Inside these may be seen crowds of the strangest composition, in every sense heterogeneous; military officers, generals and colonels, down to the lowest grade, even sergeants and corporals, sitting at the same table and staking on the same

cards ; members of Congress, Senators, Cabinet Ministers, and, upon occasions, the
Chief of the State, jostling the ragged *lepero*,
and not unfrequently standing elbow to
elbow with the footpad and salteador !—
Something stranger still, ladies compose part
of this miscellaneous assemblage ; dames of
high birth and proud bearing, but in this
carnival of cupidity not disdaining to " punt "
on the *sota* or *cavallo*, while brushing skirts
with bare-armed, bare-footed rustic damsels,
and *poblanas*, more elaborately robed, but
with scantier reputation.

After all, it is only Baden on the other
side of the Atlantic ; and it may be said
in favour of San Augustin, the fury lasts
for only a few days, instead of a whole
season.   Then the *monte* banks disappear,
with their dealers and croupiers ; the great
tents are taken down ; the gamesters gentle

and simple scatter off, most going back to the city ; and the little *pueblo* Tlalpam, resuming its wonted tranquillity, is scarce thought of till Carnival comes again.

In its normal condition, though some might deem it rather dull, it is nevertheless one of the pleasantest residential villages in the Valley. Picturesquely situated at the foot of the southern Sierras, which form a bold mountain background, it has on the other side water scenery in the curious Laguna de Xochimilco, while the grim Pedregal also approaches it, giving variety to its surroundings.

Besides its fixed population there is one that may be termed floating or intermittent ; people who come and go. These are certain " ricos " who chiefly affect its suburbs, where they have handsome houses—*casas de campo*. Not in hundreds, as at San Anjel and Tacubaya, Tlalpam being at a greater and more inconvenient distance from the capital. Still there are several around it of first-class, belonging to *familias principales*, though occupied by them only at intervals, and for a few days or weeks at a time.

One of these, owned by Don Ignacio Valverde, was a favourite place of residence with him; a tranquil retreat of which he was accustomed to avail himself whenever he could get away from his ministerial duties. Just such an interregnum had arisen some time after the stirring incidents we have recorded, and he went to stay at his San Augustin house with his daughter, the Condesa Almonté going with them as their guest. Since their last appearance before the reader, all three had passed through scenes of trial. An investigation had been gone into regarding the Callé de Plateros affair—private,

however, before Santa Anna himself, the
world not being made the wiser for it. Its
results were all in their favour, thanks to the
stern, stubborn fidelity of José who lied
like a very varlet. Such a circumstantial
story told he, no one could suspect him of
complicity in the escape of the *forzados;* far
less that his mistress, or the Condesa Almonté
had to do with it.

، Don Ignacio, too, had done his share to
hinder discovery of the truth. For, in the
end it was found necessary to take him into
the secret, the missing cloak and pistols,
with several mysterious incidents, calling for
explanation. But in making a clean breast
of it, his daughter had felt no fear of being
betrayed by him. He was not the father
to deal harshly with his child ; besides, it
was something more—a real danger. In
addition, she knew how he was affected

towards the man she had aided to escape—
that he held Don Florencio in highest esteem ;
looked upon him as a dear friend, and in a
certain tacit way had long ago signified
approval of him for a son-in-law. All these
thoughts passed through Luisa Valverde's
mind while approaching her father, and steel-
ing herself to make confession of that secret
she might otherwise have kept from him.

The result was not disappointing. Don
Ignacio consented to the deception, and they
were saved. Whatever the suspicions of
Santa Anna and his adjutant, both were
baffled about that affair, at least for the
time.

Alike had they been frustrated in their
pursuit of the *escapados*. Despite the most
zealous search through the Pedregal and
elsewhere, these could not be found, nor
even a trace of them. Still they were not

given up. Every town and village in the valley, in the mountains around, and the country outside were visited by soldiers or spies—every spot like to harbour the fugitives. Pickets were placed everywhere and patrols despatched, riding the roads by night as by day, all proving abortive.

After a time, however, this vigorous action became relaxed. Not that they who had dictated were less desirous of continuing it ; but because a matter of more importance than mere personal spite or vengeance was soon likely to declare itself, and threaten their own safety. Talk was beginning to be heard, though only in whispers, and at a far distance from the capital, of a new *pronunciamento* in preparation. And in making counter - preparations, the Dictator had now enough to occupy all his energies ; not knowing the day or the hour he might again hear the cry he so dreaded, " Patria y Libertad ".

Meanwhile the people had ceased to speak of the stirring episode which had occurred in the Calle de Plateros ; thought strange only from the odd circumstances attendant, and the fact of two of the fugitives being *Tejanos*. The city of Mexico has its daily newspapers, and on the morning after a full account of it appeared in *El Diario* and *El Monitor*. For all it was but the topic of a week ; in ten days no more heard of it ; in a month quite forgotten, save by those whom it specially concerned. So varied are the events, so frequent the changes, so strange the " Cosas de Mexico ! "

CHAPTER XLVII.

OVER THE CLIFF.

OR some time after their arrival at
the old monastery, neither Kearney
nor Cris Rock saw aught of their
late "fourth fellow" prisoner—the hunchback. They cared not to inquire after him;
the Texan repeating himself by saying;—
"This chile don't want ever to sit eyes on
his ugly pictur agin". They supposed that
he was still there, however, somewhere about
the building.

And so was he, with a chain attached to his leg, the same he had shared with Rock, its severed end now padlocked to a ring bolt; and the apartment he occupied had as much of the prison aspect as any cell in the Acordada. No doubt, in days gone by, many a refractory brother had pined and done penance therein for breach of monastic discipline.

Why the misshapen creature was so kept needs little explanation; for the same reason as prompted to bringing him thither. Helpless as he might appear, he was not harmless; and Don Ruperto knew that to restore him to liborty would be to risk losing his own, with something more. Though safely bestowed, however, no severity was shown him. He had his meals regularly, and a bed to sleep on; if but a pallet; quite as good as he had been accustomed to. Moreover, after some time

had elapsed he was relieved from this close
confinement during the hours of the day. A
clever actor, and having a tongue that could
" wheedle with the devil," he had wheedled
with the mayor-domo to granting him certain
indulgences ; among them being allowed to
spend part of his time in the kitchen and
scullery. Not in idleness, however, but occupied with work for which he had proved
himself well qualified. It was found that he
had once been " boots " in a *posado*, which
fitted him for usefulness in many ways.

In the *cocina* of the old convent his temper
was sorely tried, the other " mozos " making
cruel sport of him. But he bore it with a
meekness very different to what he had shown
while in the Acordada.

Thus acquitting himself, Gregorio, who had
him in special charge, began to regard him as
a useful if not ornamental addition to his

domestic staff of the establishment. Notwithstanding, the precaution was still continued
of locking him at night and re-attaching the
chain to his ankle. This last was more
disagreeable than aught else he had to endure.
He could bear the jibes of his fellow-scullions,
but that fetter sorely vexed him; as night
after night he was accustomed to say to the
mayor-domo as he was turning the key in its
clasp,

"It's so uncomfortable, Señor Don Gregorio," was his constantly recurring formula.
"Keeps me from sleeping, and's very trouble-
some when I want to turn over, as I often do
on account of the pains in my poor humped
shoulders. Now, why need you put it on?
Surely you're not afraid of me trying to get
away? Ha, ha! that would be turning one's
back upon best friends, *Cascaras!* I fare too
well here to think of changing quarters.

3—4

Above all going into the Acordada ; where I'd
have to go sure, if I were to show my face in
the city again.    Oh, no, Señor ! you don't
catch me leaving this snug crib, so long's you
allow me to board and bed in it.    Only I'd
like you to let me off from that nasty thing.
It's cold too ; interferes with my comfort
generally.    Do, good Don Gregorio !    For this
one night try me without it.    And if you're
not satisfied with the result then put it on ever
after, and I won't complain, I promise you."

In somewhat similar terms he had made
appeals for many nights in succession, but
without melting the heart of the " Good
Don Gregorio ".

At length, however, it proved effectual.
Among various other avocations he had
been a *Zapartero*, of the class cobbler, and
on a certain day did service to the mayor-
domo by mending his shoes.    For which

he received payment in the permisson to pass that night without being discommoded by the chain.

"It's so very kind of you, Don Gregorio !" he said, when made aware of the grace to be given to him. "I ought to sleep sound this night anyhow. But whether I do or not, I shall pray for you before going to bed all the same, *Buenas noches !*"

It was twilight outside, but almost total darkness within the cell, as the mayor-domo turned to go out of it. Otherwise he might have seen on the dwarf's features an expression calculated to make him repent his act of kindness, and instantly undo it. Could he have divined the thoughts at that moment passing through Zorillo's mind, the clasp would have quickly closed around the latter's leg, despite all gratitude due to him for the patching of the shoes.

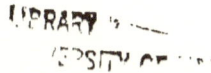

" If I can get out," he commenced in mental soliloquy, as the foot-fall of the mayor-domo died away in the distant corridor, " out, and away from them, my fortune's made ; all sorts of good things in store for me. From this time forth I need'nt fear to present myself at the door of the Acordada ; walk right into it. No danger of Don Pedro keeping me there now. Instead, I should be sent out again with a free pardon and a full purse. *Chingara;* talk of a cat in the cupboard : here are a score of them—half a hundred ! And when I let them out— aha ! "

He paused ; then rising to his feet, moved across to the door, and laid his ear against it to listen. He heard sounds, but they were sounds of merriment—the counterfeit monks at their evening meal—and did not concern him.

" What a bit of luck it may turn out after all, my getting coupled to that great brute and brought here ! That is if all goes well, and I can give them the slip. First, to make sure about the possibility of getting out of this hole. *Carrai!* I may be counting my chickens in the eggs."

Leaving the door, he glided across to the window, and set himself square against it, as if to measure its breadth by that of his own body. It was but a slit, unglazed, a single iron bar, placed vertically, dividing the aperture into two. Without removing this he could not possibly pass through. But he had the means to remove it ; that file, already known to the reader, which he had contrived to get possession of, and for days kept secret in his cell. First, however, he must see whether it was worth while using it ; for during all the time of his being there he had never been allowed an opportunity to approach the window and look out.

Leaning forward into the recess, he thrust his head between the bar and jamb, so far out as to give him a view of the ground below. This was solid rock, the crest of a steep slope, from which the wall rose as above a buttress. But there was a ledge, some ten or twelve feet under the sill, narrow, but wide enough to afford footing, which led off to more level ground. How was he to reach it ?

He knew or he would not have acted as he now did. For without spending another second in the survey, he drew back from the window, plunged his hand under his bed mat, drew forth the file, and commenced rasping away at the bar. Not noisily or in any excited haste. Even if the obstacle were removed, the time had not come for his attempt to pass out. He would wait for an hour after midnight, when all had gone to their beds.

Eaten with rust, the iron was easily sawed through, a clean cut being made near its lower end. Then, laying aside the file, and grasping the bar, he wrenched it out of the solderings. If diminutive in body, his arms were sinewy and strong as those of a coalheaver.

This task accomplished, he turned to his pallet and taking up the old blanket allowed him for a covering, began to tear it into strips. He meant to make a rope of it to lower himself down outside. But finding it quite rotten, and doubting whether it would bear his weight, he desisted and sat for a time considering. Not long till he bethought himself of something more suitable for his purpose —the chain.

" Bah !" he exclaimed, tossing aside the rags

he had commenced splicing together, "why didn't I think of that? Well, it's not too late yet. Good three yards—long enough. And the stupid has left the key behind which fits both ends. So, Mr. Chain, considering the world of worry and trouble you've been to me it's time, and only fair, you should do me a good turn by way of recompense. After you've done it, I'll forgive you."

While muttering this quaint apostrophe, he commenced groping about over the floor—not for the chain, but the key, which he knew Gregorio had left after releasing his leg from the clasp. The mayor-domo had either forgotten, or did not think it was worth while taking it away.

Having found it, he felt his way to the ring bolt and unlocking the clasp at that end returned to the window, taking the chain with him. Having made one end fast around the stump of the bar, he lowered the other down outside, cautiously, without a tinkle of its links. And now again looking out and below, he was delighted to see that it reached within a foot or two of the ledge. All this done he once more sat down on the side of the bed, to await the hour of midnight.

But he was not long quiescent, when a thought occurring caused him to resume action;

"Why not try it now?" he mentally interrogated. "They're all in the Refectory, having a fine time of it, drinking their famous wines. Some grand occasion, I heard one of the *mozos* say. There mightn't be a better chance for me than this very minute—maybe not so good. *Carramba!* I'll risk it now."

Quickly at the words he glided back to the window, climbed up into it, and squeezing out through the aperture, let himself down on the chain, link by link, as a monkey making descent of a *lliana* in the forests of the *tierra caliente*.

Soon as he found himself safe landed he let go the chain, and after a minute or so spent in silent reconnaissance of the ledge, commenced moving off along it.

Right he was in chosing that early hour, for the way he must needs take led out into the open ground, in front of the building, where at a later one a watch would have been stationed. There was none there now, and without stop or challenge he passed on and down.

Though they had never allowed him to go outside the building, he perfectly remembered the path by which he and the others had reached it, on that memorable night after their escape from the chain-gang. He recalled the two steep slopes, one above the other, with a narrow shelf between, on which they encountered the sentinel, who had hailed, " *Quien viva ?* "

Sure to be one there now, and to such hail what answer could he make?

On this he reflected while descending the upper slope. The darkness due to the over-shadowing trees made it necessary for him to go slowly, so giving him time. But it did not hinder his keeping to the path. With his long arms like the tentacles of an octopus he was able to direct his course, now and then using them to grasp over-hanging branches, or the parasites dependant therefrom. Withal he went cautiously, and so silently, that the sentinel—for sure enough one was there—heard no noise to warn him of an enemy behind. In his monkish garb, he was standing on the outer edge of the shelf rock, his face turned to the valley, which was just beginning to show silvery white under the rays of a rising moon. Perhaps, like Don Ruperto, he was gazing on some spot, a house, endeared to him as the home of his childhood; but from which, as the leader of the Free Lances, he had been bereft by the last confiscation. Possibly he was indulging in the hope of its being soon restored to him, but least of all dreaming of danger behind.

It was there, notwithstanding—in fiendish shape and close proximity. A creature squatted like a toad, human withal, saying to himself,

" What wouldn't I give for a knife with a blade six inches long ! "

Then with a sudden change of thought, seeing the chance to do without the knife, making a dash forward, with the ape-like arms extended, and pushing the sentinel over !

The cry that came from the latter on

feeling the impulse from behind, was stifled as he went swirling down to the bottom of the cliff.

## Chapter XLVIII.

## ON DOWN THE MOUNTAIN.

"DEAD!" muttered the inhuman wretch, as he stood upon the spot late occupied by his victim, looking down over the cliff. "Dead he must be; unless a man can fall two hundred feet and still live; which isn't likely. That clears the way, I take it; and unless I have the ill-luck to meet some one coming up—a straggler—it'll be all right. As sound ascends, I ought to hear them before they could see me. I shall keep my ears open."

Saying which he commenced the descent of the second slope, proceeding in the same cautious way as before.

The path was but a ledge, which, after running fifty yards in a direct line, made an abrupt double back in the opposite direction, all the while obliquing downwards. Another similar zig-zag, with a like length of declivity traversed, and he found himself at the cliff's base, among shadowy, thick standing trees. He remembered the place; and that before reaching it on their way up they had followed the trend of the cliff for more than a quarter of a mile. So taking this for his guide, he kept on along the back track.

Not far, before seeing that which brought him to a stop. If he had entertained any doubt about the sentinel being dead, it would have been resolved now. There lay the man's body among the loose rocks, not only lifeless, but shapeless. A break in the continuity of the timber let the moonlight through, giving the murderer a full view of him he had murdered.

The sentinel had fallen upon his back, and lay with his face upward, his crushed body doubled over a boulder; the blood was welling from his mouth and nostrils, and the open eyes glared ghastly in the white, weird light. It was a sight to inspire fear in the mind of an ordinary individual, even in that of a murderer. But it had no effect on this strange *lusus* of humanity, whose courage was equal to his cruelty. Instead of giving the body a wide berth, and scared-like stealing past, he walked boldly up to it, saying in apostrophe—

"So you're there! Well, you need not blame me, but your luck. If I hadn't pushed you over, you'd have shot me like a dog, or brained me with the butt of your gun. Aha! I was too much for you, Mr. Monk or soldier, which ever you were, for you're neither now."

"Just possible," he continued, changing the form of his monologue, "He may have, a purse; the which I'm sure to stand in need of before this time to-morrow. If without money his weapons may be of use to me."

With a nimbleness which bespoke him no novice at trying pockets, he soon touched the bottom of all those on the body, to find them empty.

"Bah," he ejaculated, drawing back with a disappointed air, "I might have known there was nothing in them. Whatever cash they've had up there has been spent long ago,

3—5

and their wine will soon be out too. His gun I don't care for ; besides, I see it's broken ;— yes, the stock snapped clean off. But this stiletto it's worth taking with me. Even if I shouldn't need it in the way of a weapon, it looks like a thing Mr. Pawnbroker would appreciate."

Snatching the dagger—a silver-hilted one— from the corpse of its ill-starred owner, he secreted it inside his tattered rag of a coat, and without delay proceeded on.

Soon after he came to a point where the path forsaking the cliff turned to the left, down the slope of the mountain. He knew that would take him into the Pedregal, where he did not desire to go. Besides his doubts of being able to find the way through the lava field, there was no particular need for his attempting so difficult a track. All he wanted was to get back to the city by the most direct route, and as soon as possible into the presence of a man of whom during late days he had been thinking much. For from this man he much expected, in return for a tale he could tell him. It must be told direct, and for this reason all caution was required. He might fall into hands that would not only hinder him from relating it in the right quarter, but prevent his telling it at all.

Just where the path diverged to the left going down to the Pedregal, a mass of rocks rose bare above the tops of the trees. Clambering to its summit he obtained a view of what lay below; the whole valley bathed in bright moonlight, green meadows, fields of maize, and maguey, great sheets of water with haze hanging over them, white and gauzy as a bridal veil. The city itself was distinguishable at a long distance, and in places

nearer specklings of white telling of some
*pueblita,* or single spots where stood a *rancho*
or *hacienda.* Closer still, almost under his
feet, a clump of those mottlings was more
conspicuous ; which he recognised as the
*pueblo* of San Augustin. A narrow ribbon-
like strip of greyish white passing through it,
and on to the city, he knew to be the Great
Southern or Acapulco road, which enters the
capital by the *garita* of San Antonio de Abad.
This route he decided on taking.

Having made note of the necessary bear-
ings, he slipped back down the side of the
rock, and looked about for a path leading to
the right.

Not long till he discovered one, a mere
trace made by wild animals through the
underwood—sufficiently practicable for him,
as he could work his way through any
tangle of thicket. Sprawling along it, and

rapidly, despite all obstructions, he at length came out on the Acapulco road, a wide causeway, with the moon full upon it.

The track was easy and clear even now, too clear to satisfy him. He would have preferred a darker night. San Augustin had to be passed through, and he knew that in it were both *serenos* and alguazils. Besides, he had heard the *moxos* at the monastery speak of troops stationed there, and patrols at all hours along the roads around. If taken up by these he might still hope to reach his intended destination; but neither in the time he desired, nor the way he wished. He must approach the man, with whom he meant seeking an interview, not as a prisoner but voluntarily. And he must see this man soon, to make things effectual, as the reward he was dreaming of sure.

Urged by these reflections, he made no further delay; but taking to the dusty road moved in all haste along it. In one way the moon was in his favour. The causeway was not straight, for it was still a deep descent towards the valley, and carried by zig-zags; so that at each angle he was enabled to scan the stretch ahead, and see that it was clear before exposing himself upon it. Then he would advance rapidly on the next turning point, stop again and reconnoitre.

Thus alternately making traverses and pauses, he at length reached the outskirts of the *pueblo*, unchallenged and unobserved. But the problem was how to pass through it; all the more difficult at that early hour. He had heard the church clock tolling the hours as he came down the mountain, and he knew it had not struck ten. A beautiful night, the villagers would be all abroad; and how was he to appear in the street without attracting notice—he above all men? His deformity of itself would betray him. An expression of blackest bitterness came over his features as he thus reflected. But it was not a time to indulge in sentimentalities. San Augustin must be got through somehow, if he could not find a way around it.

For this last he had been looking some time both to the right and left. To his joy, just as he caught sight of the first houses— villa residences they were, far straggling along the road—a lane running in behind them seemed to promise what he was in search of. From its direction it should enable him to turn the village, without the necessity of passing through the *plaza*, or at all entering upon the streets. Without more ado he dodged into the lane.

It proved the very sort of way he was wishing for; dark from being overshadowed with trees. A high park-like wall extended along one side of it, within which were the trees, their great boughs drooping down over.

Keeping close in to the wall he glided on, and had got some distance from the main road, when he saw that which brought him to a sudden stop—a man approaching from the opposite direction. In the dim light, the figure was as yet barely discernible, but there was a certain something in its gait— the confidential swagger of the policeman— which caught the practised eye of Zorillo, involuntarily drawing from him the muttered speech—

" *Maltida sea !* An alguazil ! "

Whether the man was this or not, he must be avoided; and, luckily for the dwarf, the means of shunning him were at hand, easy as convenient. It was but to raise his long arms above his head, lay hold of one of the overhanging branches, and draw himself up to the top of the wall; which he did upon the instant. It was a structure of *adobés*, with a coping quite a yard in width, and laid flat along this, he was altogether invisible, to one passing below.

The man, alguazil or not, neither saw him nor suspected his being there, but walked tranquilly on.

When he was well beyond ear-shot, the dwarf deeming himself safe, was about to drop back into the lane, when a murmur of voices prompted him to keep his perch. They were feminine, sweet as the sound of rippling brooks, and gradually becoming more distinct; which told him that from whom they proceeded were approaching the spot. He had already observed that the enclosure was a grand ornamental garden with walks, fountains and flowers ; a large house on its further side.

Presently the speakers appeared—two young ladies sauntering side by side along one of the walks, the soft moonlight streaming down upon them. As it fell full upon their faces, now turned toward the wall, the dwarf started at a recognition, inwardly exclaiming :—

" *Santissima !*—The senoritas of the carriage !"

Chapter XLIX.

A TALE OF STARVATION.

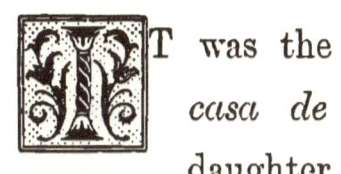T was the garden of Don Ignacio's *casa de campo*; the ladies, his daughter and the Condesa. The lovely night, with balm in the air and a bright moon shining through the sky, had drawn them out, and they strolled through the grounds, keeping step, as it were, to that matchless melody, the song of the *czenzontle*. But note of no nightingale was in their

thoughts, which were engrossed by graver themes.

" 'Tis so strange our never hearing from them, and not a word of them. What do you make of it. Ysabel ? Is it a bad sign ?"

The question was asked by the Dona Luisa.

" That we have'nt heard *from* them is—in a way," responded the Countess. " Yet that may be explained, too. The probability is from the roads being all watched and guarded, as we know they are, they'd be cautious about communicating with us. If they've sent a messenger—which I hope they have'nt—he must have been intercepted and made prisoner. And, then, the message ; that might compromise us. But I know Ruperto will be careful. Not to have heard *of* them is all for the best—the very best. It should almost assure us that they're still free, and safe somewhere. Had they been recaptured we'd have known before this. All Mexico would be talking about it."

"True," assented Don Ignacio's daughter, with a feeling of relief. "They cannot have been retaken. But I wonder where they are now."

"So I myself, Lusita. I hope, however, not at that old monastery of which Ruperto gave me a description in one of his letters. It's somewhere up in the mountains. But with the country all around so occupied by troops it would seem an unsafe place. I trust they've got over the Sierra, and down to Acapulco. If they have, we needn't feel so very anxious about them."

"Why not, Ysabel ?"

"Why not. Ah ! that's a question you haven't yet come to understand. But never mind the reason now. You'll know it in good time ; and when you do, I've no fear but you'll be satisfied ; your father too."

Don Ignacio's daughter was both puzzled
and surprised at the strange words.  But she
knew the Countess had strange ways ; and,
though a bosom friend, was not without some
secrets she kept to herself.  This was one of
them, no doubt, and she forebore pressing for
an explanation.

What the Condesa hinted at was that
disaffection in the south, the expected *pronunciamento*, which, if successful, would not
only depose the Dictator, but of course also
his Cabinet Ministers, her friend's father
among them.  With some knowledge of coming events, she declined imparting this to
the Dona Luisa through delicacy.  Right
was she, also, in her surmise as to the
messenger ; none had been intercepted, none
having been sent out, just for the reason
surmised by her.

They had made a turn or two of the

grounds, thus conversing, when both came
to a sudden stop. Simultaneously uttering
exclamations of alarm, "*Santissima!*" and
"*Madre de Dios!*"

"What can it be?" gasped Dona Luisa.
"Is it a man?"

No wonder she should so doubtingly inter-
rogate, since her question referred to that
strange creature on the top of the wall,
seeming more ape than human being.

That he was human, however, was to be
proved by his being gifted with the power
of speech, put forth on the instant after.
Before the Countess could make answer to
the question (of course overheard by him),
he interposed, saying—

"Pray, don't be alarmed, your ladyships,
at a poor, miserable creature like me. I
know that my body is anything but
shapely; but my soul—that I trust is dif-

ferent. But, Senoritas, surely you remember me ? "

While speaking, he had raised himself into an upright attitude, and the moonlight falling upon him showed his shape in all its grotesqueness of outline. This, with his words, at once recalled their having seen him before. Yes ; it was the *enano*, whom the big Texan had swung up to the box of their carriage.

Astonishment hindering reply to his interrogatory, he continued :

" Well, your ladyships, I'm sorry you don't recognise me ; the more from my being one of your best friends, or, at all events, the friend of your friends."

" Of whom do you speak, sir ? " asked the Countess, first to recover composure, the Dona Luisa echoing the interrogatory. Both were alike anxious for the answer, better than half divining.

"Two worthy gentlemen, who, like my poor self, had the misfortune to get shut up in the Acordada; more than that, set to work in the filthy sewers. Thanks to the luck of your ladyship's carriage coming past at a convenient time, we all escaped; and so far have been successful in eluding the search that's been made for us."

"You have succeeded—all?" both asked in a breath, their eagerness throwing aside reserve.

"Oh! yes; as I've said, so far. But it's been hard times with us in our hiding place; so hard, indeed, we might well have wished ourselves back in the prison."

"How so, sir? Tell us all! You needn't fear to speak out: we'll not betray you."

"*Por Dios!* I'm not afraid of your lady-ships doing that. Why should I, since I'm here on account of your own friends, and on an errand of mercy?"

"An errand of mercy?"

3—6

" Yes. And one of necessity as well. Ah! that far more."

" Go on, sir ! Please tell us what it is ! "

" Well, Señoritas, I've been deputed on a foraging expedition. For we're in a terrible strait—all four of us. You may remember there were four."

" We do. But, how in a terrible strait ? "

" How ! Why, for want of food ; starving. Up in the mountains, where we've been hiding for now nearly a month, all we've had to live upon was wild fruits and roots ; often eating them raw, too. We daren't any of us venture down, as the roads all round have been beset by spies and soldiers. It's only in sheer desperation I've stolen through them ; the Señor Don Ruperto sending me to San Augustin in the hope I might be able to pick up some provisions. I was just slipping the village the back way, when an alguazil coming along made it necessary for me to climb up here and hide myself. The unlucky part of it all is, that even if I get safe in, I haven't the wherewith to buy the eatables, and must beg them. That I fear won't be easy ; people are so hard-hearted."

For a time his surprised listeners stood silent, giving way to sad reflections. Florencio and Ruperto starving !

" May I hope," continued the lying wretch, "your ladyships will let me look upon this accidental encounter as a God-send, and that you will give me something to buy——"

" O, sir ! " interrupted the Countess, " we will give you that. Luisa, have you any money in your purse ? I haven't in mine— nothing to signify."

" Nor I either—how unfortunate ! We must——"

" Never mind money, your ladyships ;

money's worth will do quite as well. A *reloja*, rings, anything in the way of jewellery. I chance to know a place in the village where I can convert them into cash."

" Here, take this ! " cried the Countess, handing him her watch, the same which had been hypothecated to José, but redeemed by a money payment.

" And this ! " said the Dona Luisa, also holding out a watch, both of which he speedily took possession of.

" 'Tis very generous of your ladyships," he said, stowing them away among his rags, " the proceeds of these ought to support us for a long time, even allowing for the reduced rate I'll have to accept from the pawnbroker. Afterwards we must do the best we can."

As he spoke his little sparkling eyes were avariciously bent upon certain other objects he saw scintillating in the moonlight—bracelets, rings upon their fingers and in their ears. The hint was hardly needed. Enough for them the thought that more help might be required by those dear to them, and at a time when they could not extend it.

In less than five minutes after both had divested themselves of every article in the way of gold, or gems, adorning them. They even plucked the pendants from their ears, thrusting all indiscriminately into the outstretched hands of the hunchback.

" *Gracias!—mil gracias!* " he ejaculated, crowding everything into his pocket. " But your ladyships will scarce care to accept thanks from me. 'Twill be more to your satisfaction to know that your generosity will be the saving of valuable lives, two of them, if I mistake not, very dear to you. Oh! won't the Señores Don Ruperto and Don Florencio be delighted at the tale I shall take back—the

Virgin seeing me safe! Not for the provisions I may carry, but how I obtained the means of purchasing them. But as time's pressing, Senorita, I won't say a word more, only *Adios!*"

Without waiting for permission to depart or rejoinder of any kind, he slipped down from the wall, and disappeared on its other side.

It was an abrupt leave-taking, which alike surprised and disappointed them. For they had many questions to ask, and intended asking him—many anxieties they wished set at rest.

CHAPTER L.

AN ENCOUNTER WITH OLD
ACQUAINTANCES.

ASSING out of the San Augustin towards the city, the great National Road, as already said, touches upon the Pedregal, the lava rocks here and there rising cliff-like over it. On the other side are level meadows stretching to the shore of the Laguna de Xochimilco; this last overgrown with a lush acquatic

vegetation called the *cinta*, at a distance
appearing more pastureland than lake.
Excellent pasturage is afforded on the strip
between; that end of it adjacent to the
*pueblo* being apportioned among several
of the rich proprietors of villas, who turn
their household stock upon it, as milch kine,
and horses kept for the saddle or carriage.

Just about the time when the hunchback
was abruptly bidding "Adios" to the ladies,
a man might have been seen moving along
this part of the road at some half mile
distance from the skirts of the village, with
face turned cityward. But that he had no
intention of journeying so far was evident
both by his gait and the character of his
dress. He was going at a slow walk, now
and then loitering, as if time was of little
consequence. Morever, he was in his shirt
sleeves, and without the universal *serape*,

which often serves for both cloak and coat. Otherwise his garb was the ordinary stable wear of a Mexican gentleman's servant; wide velveteen trousers open along the outer seams, and fended with leather at breech and bottoms. "Batos" and a black glaze hat completed his habiliments, with a scarf of China crape, the *chammora*, around his waist. Scanning the face shadowed by the broad rim of his *sombrero*, it was seen to be that of José, Don Ignacio's groom; while his errand along that road could be guessed, by seeing what he carried over his arm—a couple of slip halters. The horses, for whom they were intended, were to be seen standing at a gate, a little further, having browsed their fill; a pair of greys, recognisable as the famous *frisones;* all the easier now from one of them showing a split ear. They had been turned out to cool

their hooves on the soft meadow sward, and
he was on his way to take them back to
their stable.

Along the other side of the road, for a
stretch of some distance, extended the Pedregal, forming a low ridge with a precipitous
face towards the causeway. As the *cochero*
got up to where his pets were expecting him,
he saw a *coyote* standing upon the crest cliff,
just opposite the horses, in an attitude and
with an air as if it had been holding conversation with them. Solely for frolic's sake, he
made a rush towards it, giving a swoop and
swinging the halters around his head. Of
course, the afrighted animal turned tail, and
retreated ; instantly disappearing from his
sight.

The little spurt had carried him in under
the shadow of the rocks ; and as he faced
round to recross the moonlit causeway, he saw

.

coming along it that which, by some mysterious instinct, prompted him to keep his place.
After all, no mystery about it; for in the
diminutive, crab-like form seen approaching,
he recognised the dwarf-hunchback who had
shared the box seat with him on that day
never to be forgotten.

Nothing had been heard of the creature,
since, so far as José knew; and, therefore, it
might be supposed his appearance would have
been welcome, promising some news of those
with whom he had been last seen. But so far
from the *cochero* stepping out into the road to
receive him, he but drew closer to the cliff,
where an embayment in black shadow promised
him perfect concealment.

Soon after Zorillo came shuffling along
through the dust, keeping close to the shaded
side of the road. Having cleared the skirts of
the village, however, he was less careful now.

Not likely there would be anyone abroad at that hour—for it had gone ten—but if so, there was the Pedregal alongside, to which he could retreat. Evidently he had not seen José, as when first seen himself he was turning a corner, and the other had been for some time in shadow.

When nearly opposite the meadow gate he also made a stop, with a start, at perceiving the two horses' heads stretched over it, one with a cleft ear! His start came through recognition of them.

"Oho!" he exclaimed, "you there, too, my noble *frisones?* *Caspita?* this is meeting one's old acquaintances all in a heap! It now only needs to encounter *cochero,* and the party will be complete! Well, I may live in hope to see him too, sometime; and won't there be a reckoning when we're altogether again?"

He was about to pass on, when a clattering

of hoofs were heard behind, in the direction of the *pueblo,* as if horsemen were issuing out of it.  Shortly after, a dark clump was seen rounding the corner, and coming on along the white ribband of road.  The sabres clanking against stirrup-irons proclaimed it a cavalry troop.

Like a tarantula retreating to its tree-cave, the dwarf darted in under the cliff, there crouching down—so close to José that the latter could have almost touched him with the tips of his fingers.  He had no desire to do so, no thought of it; but the very opposite.  His wish was to avoid an encounter; and good reason for it, as he was soon after made aware.  Fortunately for him, the hunchback neither saw nor had a suspicion of his proximity.  With face turned to the road, he was altogether occupied with the party approaching.

The Hussars turned out—an escort of some eight or ten files, with two officers at its head, these riding side by side and a little in advance. They were chatting gaily and rather vociferously; the voice of him who spoke loudest being well known to José. For Colonel Santander, whether welcome or not, was a frequent visitor at the *casa de campo* of Don Ignacio Valverde. And the dwarf now remembered it too, as he did so abandoning all attempt at concealment and gliding out into the middle of the road.

"*Carajo!*" simultaneously shouted the two officers, as their horses reared up, snorting at the strange shape so suddenly presented before them. "What the *Demonio* is it, if not Satan himself?" added Santander.

"No, *Señor Coronel*," returned Zorillo. "Not the devil; only a poor creature whom God has cursed by making him in a shape that isn't altogether fashionable. But just for that reason I trust being recalled to your Excellency's remembrance—am I not?"

"Ah! You were in the Acordada?"

"*Si, Señor Coronel.*"

"And 'twas you I saw coupled to the Tejano?"

"The same, Señor. In that prosecuted by a like ill no doubt, the devil all the time directing it."

"But where have you been, since, sirrah?"

"Ah! *Excellenza!* that's just it; the very thing I want to tell you. I was on my way to the city in hopes of obtaining an interview with you. What a bit of fortune you passing here; 'twill save me a journey I was ill able to make; for I'm quite worn out, and weak, from being starved up there in the mountains."

"Oh! you've been up there?"

"Yes, Señor Coronel, in hiding with the

others. But not like them voluntarily. They took me along with them, whether I would or no, and have kept me ever since— till this night, when an opportunity offered for giving them the slip. It isn't all of four hours since I parted company with them. But if your Excellency wishes to hear the whole story, perhaps you'd like it better in private. If I mistake not, some of it should only reach your own ears."

Santander had been already thinking of this, and turning to the officer by his side, he said :

" Take the men on, Ramirez. Halt at a hundred yards or so, and wait for me."

In obedience to the order the escort moved on, stopping as directed, the dialague between Santander and the dwarf meanwhile continuing. It was more of a monologue, the latter giving a detailed relation of all that had occurred to him since the time of their escape from the chain-gang, with comments and suggestions added.

After hearing all, Santander rose in his stirrups, his features showing triumph, such as Satan might feel at a world of souls just delivered to him.

" The game is mine at last !" he muttered to himself, " every trick of it. They're in a trap now ; and when they go out of it, 'twill be to the *garrota.*"

For a moment he sat silent, apparently considering what was his best course to pursue. Then, seemingly having decided, he call out—

" Ramirez ! Send a couple of men to me— the corporal and another."

These, detached from the escort, came trotting back along the road.

" Here, *cabo !* Take charge of this curious

3—7

specimen. Keep him here, and see that you hold him safe till you have my orders for releasing him. Don't stray from this spot as you value your own neck—not an inch."

Saying which he put spurs to his horse, and rejoined his escort. Then commanding, "Forward! at the double quick!" they started off at full gallop towards the city.

## CHAPTER LI.

## A GRUMBLING GUARD.

ART of the dialogue between Santander and the hunchback was
overheard by José; enough of it
to give him the trembles. Among its revelations was nought relating to himself, or his
connivance at the escape of the prisoners.
For all, he could see that he was now in as
much danger as they who were in hiding.
The Colonel of Hussars had gone on to the

city, perhaps to complete some duty already
engaging him, but as likely to obtain a
stronger force. And as his words told, he
would return again ; and no doubt make
direct for the old monastery, the dwarf guiding him.

The first thought of the faithful *cochero*
was not about himself, nor his horses. These
might stay in the meadow all night as they
were now likely to do. The lives of men
were at stake—his own among the number—
and his sole purpose now was to get home,
report what he had heard to his young mistress and the Condesa ; then hasten up the
mountain to warn the imperilled ones. As
good luck would have it, he knew the place
they were in. Son of a *carbonero*, when a
boy he had helped his father in the charcoal
burning business ; was familiar with the
mountain forests, and their paths, and had

more than once been at the abandoned
monastery. He could easily find the way
to it. But the difficulty was to get back to
his master's house—even stir from the spot
on which he stood. Soon as receiving their
orders the two hussars had dismounted, and
tied up their horses, one on each side of the
rocky embayment; they themselves, with
their curious charge, occupying the space between. It was not possible to pass without
being seen by them, and as surely seized.

So long as he kept his place he might feel
comparatively safe. The cove was of a three-
cornered shape, with luckily a deep dark cleft
at its inner angle, into which he had already
squeezed himself. While the moon remained
low, and the cliff made shadow, there was
little likelihood of their seeing him unless
they came close up. Still the situation was
aught but pleasant, and ere long became

irksome in the extreme ; the conversation to which he was compelled to listen making it so.

The two *husares* did not seem to be in the best of temper ; the corporal more especially showing signs of dissatisfaction. Groping about for a stone to seat himself on, he grumbled out :—

" *Maddita!* What a bore, having to stay here till they get back. Heaven knows when that will be. Like enough not before morning. I thought we were going to pass the night in San Augustin, and had hopes of a chat with that *muchachita* at the house where the colonel visits."

" Pepita, you mean—lady's maid to the Dona Luisa Valverde ? "

" Of course, I mean her, the pretty dear : and have reason to think she is a bit sweet upon me."

José's heart was on fire—his blood boiling. It was with difficulty he restrained himself from springing out upon the soldier and clutching him by the throat. He succeeded, however, in keeping his place, if not his temper; for it would have been sheer madness to show himself there and then. What came after quite tranquillised him.

"Well, *cabo*," returned he of the rank and file, seemingly without fear of speaking plain to the non-commissioned officer. "I should be sorry to dash your hopes; but as a friend I can't help saying, I don't think you have much chance in that quarter. She's a step higher, that same Pepita; holds her head far above any of us common soldiers——"

"Common soldiers! I'm a corporal; you forget that, *hombre*. But why do you think my chances are so poor?"

"Because I've heard say there's a man

about the establishment to whom she's already
given what heart she may have had to give—
that they're engaged. The fellow's groom or
*cochero*, or something of the sort."

José breathed easier now, noways provoked
at having been spoken of as a " fellow ".

" Bah ! " contemptuously exclaimed the
corporal. " What care I for that horse-
cleaner and carriage-washer for a rival ! I've
cut out scores of such before now, and will
do the same with him. Lie down there, you
devil's imp ! " he added, turning savagely
upon the dwarf, and venting his spleen by
giving the creature a kick. " Down, or I'll
break every bone in your body."

" Mercy, master ! " expostulated the hunchback. " Don't be so cruel to a fellow creature."

" Fellow-creature. That's good, ha—ha—
ha ! " and the brute broke into a hoarse laugh,
till the rocks echoed his fiendish cachination.

"Well, your worship," rejoined he thus inhumanly mocked, with an air of assumed meekness; "whatever I am, it pains me to think I should be the cause of keeping you here. But why should you stay, may 1 ask? You don't suppose I'm going to run away? If I were with you as a prisoner; but I am not. I sought an interview with your Colonel of my own free will. Surely you saw that!"

"True enough, he did," interposed the soldier.

"And what if he did," growled the corporal.

"Only, Señor, to show that I have no intention to part company with you, nor wish neither. *Por Dios!* don't let me hinder you from having that chat with the *muchachita*. It's but a step back to the *pueclo*, and like as not she'll be on the look out for you, spite of what your comrade says. Maybe he has an eye to the pretty dear himself, and that's why he wishes to discourage you."

As this rigmarole was delivered in the most comical manner, it put the soldiers in a better humour, both breaking out into laughter.

Of course the corporal had no thought of availing himself of the permission so accorded. Their orders were strict to stay in that spot, and stay they must. The question was how were they to spend the time.

A smoke to begin with; and they drew out their cigarritos, with flint, steel, and tinder.

Soon as the red coal appeared beneath their noses, said the *cabo* to his comrade:

"By the way, Perico, have you your cards with you?"

"Did you ever know me to be without them?"

" How lucky! I quite forgot mine."

" That's because your mind was bent upon Pepita. I saw you giving your moustache an extra twist this evening."

" Oh! bother Pepita. Let's have an *albur* of monté."

" How about light ? "

" The moon's clear enough, if it was'nt we could manage with our cigars. Many's the game I've played that way."

" All right! But the stakes? I haven't a *cuartilla*—nay not so much as a *claco*."

" *Carramba!* Nor I either. I spent the last on a drink just before we got into the saddle. It's bad; but we can bet upon the credit system, and use cartridges for counters, Ah, stay !"

At which he turned his eyes upon the dwarf, with a look of peculiar significance, cupidity the prevailing expression.

The latter saw it with a heaviness of heart, and a shuddering throughout his frame. All the time apprehensive about the plunder with which his pockets were crammed, he instinctively anticipated what was coming.

## CHAPTER LII.

## A DANAE'S SHOWER.

"NOW, I shouldn't wonder," continued the corporal, shifting upon his seat, and facing fully round to the dwarf; "I shouldn't at all wonder but that this diminutive gentleman has some spare cash upon him; and maybe he'll oblige us by a little loan, considering the occasion. What say you, *Señor Enano?*"

"I haven't any," was the ready answer. "And sorry to say it too—that I am."

" It don't look much like he has," observed Perico, with a glance at the hunchback's tattered habiliments.

" Looks are not always to be relied on," persisted the corporal. " Who'd ever suspect a pearl inside an ugly oyster-shell ? "

" I haven't, indeed, *Señor Cabo*," once more protested the dwarf with earnest emphasis. " If I had, you'd be welcome to the loan you speak of. No man likes a game of *monté* better than myself. Alas ! so far from being in funds, I'm too like your worships—without a *claco*. I've been stripped of everything ; and, if you knew my story, you'd pity me, I'm sure."

" What story ? " demanded the *cabo* becoming curious.

" Why, that I've been robbed of all the money I had. It wasn't much to be sure, only two *pesetas* and a *real*, but still that was better than empty pockets. It happened about half-an-hour ago. I was on my way to San Augustin, thinking I'd there get some supper, with a night's lodging ; when not far from this, two men—footpads I suppose they were—rushed out from the roadside, and made straight at me. One took the right, the other left. But I've good long arms, as you see, pretty strong too ; and so I was able to keep them off for a while. Several times they caught hold of my wrists ; but I suc- ceeded in jerking them free again. I believe I could have wrestled them both, but that one getting angry, pulled out a long-bladed knife, and threatened to cut my throat with it. *Por dios!* I had to surrender then, seeing he was in earnest."

While giving this somewhat prolix account of an altogether imaginary adventure, he had started to his feet, and accompanied his speech with a series of pantomimic gestures; dancing and flinging his arms about, as he professed to have done while defending himself against the footpads. The grotesqueness of the performance, though seen only in the dim light—for he kept under the shadow—set his listeners to laughing. Little dreamt they why he was treating them to the spectacle, or how cleverly he was outwitting them.

But there was a third spectator of the scene, unknown to all of them, who was aware of it. The *cochero* could not at first tell what were the things striking him in the pit of the stomach, as if he was being pelted with pebbles! But he could see they came from the hands of the hunchback, flung behind in his repeated contortions and gesticulations. Moreover, that they glistened while passing through the air, and looked whitish where they lay, after falling at his own feet.

"Well; what did they do to you then?" asked the corporal when he and his comrade had finished their guffaw. "Stripped you clean, as you've said?"

"*Ay, Dios!* Just that, Señor. Took everything I had except the rags I wear; and to them I might well have made them welcome."

"Now, are you sure they took everything?" questioned the other, still suspicious. The earnestness of the dwarf's affirmation made him so.

"Of course, Señor. Quite sure. I'll swear to it, if you like."

"Oh, there's no need for the formality of an oath. Simpler to search you! and more satisfactory. Draw up here in front of me!"

The hunchback obeyed with an air of confident alacrity. He had no reluctance to being searched now, knowing his pockets were

3—8

empty. Of which the searcher satisfied himself by groping about among the rags, and sounding every receptable where coin might be kept.

But if he found no money, an article turned up, which no little surprised himself and his comrade—a stiletto !

" *Caspita !*" he exclaimed, as his hand touched something hard in the waistband of the dwarf's breeches, stuck behind his back. " What have we here ?  As I live a dagger !" drawing it out and holding it to the light. " Silver hilted, too ! Yes ; its silver, sure ; and blade beautifully chased—worth a *doblone* at the very least !"

" Half mine," interrupted Perico, putting in his claim.

" All right, *camardo*.  We'll settle that by-and-bye.  Now, you limb of Satan !" he continued to the hunchback, " you told us the footpads had stripped you clean. How do you explain this ?"

" Easily enough, your worship. They only thought of trying in my pockets, and the stiletto being there behind where you've found it, luckily they overlooked it."

" Oh ! indeed ;" doubtingly rejoined the corporal; " and pray how did you become possessed of it, *Señor Enano!* A dagger worth a *doblone* isn't a likely thing for such as you to be owner of—that is, in an honest way.

" I admit, your worship, it isn't likely. For all, I came honestly by the article. It's an heirloom in our family ; belonged to my great-great-grandfather, and's descended through several generations. For know, Señor, my ancestors were not deformed like poor me. Some of them were gallant soldiers, as yourself. Indeed, one of them rose to the rank of sergeant—that was my mother's grandfather ; but this dagger didn't come down from him, being left in the main line."

" Well," laughingly returned the corporal, after listening to the quaint chapter of explanations, " the future herald of our family won't have to trace it beyond yourself. You're now under our protection, and have no need to warlike weapons. So we, your protectors, will take the liberty of appropriating the historical toy. Get out the cards, Perico ! Let us see whether it is to be yours or mine."

" *May bueno !* " responded Perico. " How will you have the game ? A single *albur* or two out of three ? "

" Well, as we've only the one stake, and no end of time for winning and loosing it, we'd better make it the long game."

" All right—come on ! I have the cards

spread—*sota y caballo.* How sweet the
Queen's face looks in the moonlight ! Ah !
she's smiling at me, I know, as good as to
say — 'Worthy Perico, that silver-handled
weapon, your corporal tells you is worth all
of an *onza,* will ere long be thine '."

"Well, lay on the Queen if you like. I'll
go the Jack, with all his grinning. Now
shuffle, and deal off."

By this the two had seated themselves,
*vis-a-vis,* just outside the verge where met
moonlight and shadow, a suite of cards
turned face up between them, the dealing
pack in the hands of Perico. The hunchback, on his knees, with neck craned out,
was a spectator ; but one whose thoughts
were not with his eyes. Instead, dwelling
upon the valuables he had so cunningly
chucked back, making the mental calculation
as to how much they might be damaged by

breakage, but caring less for that than the danger of their also becoming stakes in that game of *monte*. Could he have known what was going on behind, he would possibly have preferred it so.

The unseen spectator, though silent, was not inactive ; but the reverse. From the moment of seeing himself shut up,—as it were, in a penn—he had given all his thoughts to how he might escape out of it. It needed none to tell him there was no chance frontwards by the road. A rush he might make past the two soldiers, risking seizure, and surely having the bullets of their carbines sent after him. But even though he got off in that way, what would be the upshot ? The hunchback would be certain to recognise him, remembering all. Knowing, too, that his dialogue with the Hussar colonel must have been overheard, he would hasten the very event which he, José,

was now all anxious to provide against. The
word of warning meant for those now so much
needing it might reach them too late.

All these thoughts had passed through the
*cochero's* mind before the card-playing commenced. More, too, for he had carefully
inspected the cliff overhead, so far as the light
would allow, aided by groping. To his joy he
had discovered that there was a possibility of
scaling it. A sharp pinnacle of rock was
within reach of the swing of his halters; and
skilled in the use of the *laso*, over this he had
succeeded in flinging the headstall of one,
hooking it fast. It but remained to swarm up
the rope : and he was watching for an opportunity, when glittering golden things, like a
Danae's shower, came raining against his ribs,
to fall at his feet.

He saw no reason for these being left to lie
there, but a good one against it ; so, stooping

cautiously forward, he gathered up all, stowing them away in his pockets. Then turning and taking hold of the halter, with as little noise as possible, he hoisted himself up to the crest of the cliff.

The soldiers engrossed with their game, and the dwarf, though but a spectator, having also become interested in it—none of the three either saw or heard him. And the last he heard of them as he stole silently away, was the corporal delightedly calling out,

" *Sota en la puerta, mozo !* The dagger's mine, darling Perico !"

## Chapter LIII.

## A SERIES OF SURPRISES.

HE *cochero* had but a confused idea of what he was carrying away with him. By the feel, watches, with chains and bracelets; besides some smaller articles wrapped in bits of papers. The uncertainty of his getting safe up the cliff hindered him from giving them even the most cursory examination, nor did he think of doing this till at sufficient distance from the card-playing party to feel sure he was beyond danger of pursuit. Then the temptation to have a look at the things, which had so strangely and un-expectedly come into his possession, became irresistible ; and sitting down upon a ledge of rock, he drew them out into the light of the moon. Two watches there were, both gold, and one with a jewelled case.

" *Carrai !* " he exclaimed, as his eyes fell upon the latter, and became fixed in a stare of blank amazement ; " Can it be ! It is—the Condesa's watch—the very one she would have given me ! But how came the hunch-back to have it ? Surely he must have stolen it. The other, too, with all these things !"

He looked at the second watch, but as it had never been in his hands before, he was unable to identify it. Still it resembled one he had seen his mistress wearing, and most likely was the same.

The bracelets, chains, necklets, and brooches would be theirs, too; as also the rings and other bijouterie, which the dwarf had found time to do up in paper.

"Stolen them?" continued the *cochero*, interrogatively, as he ran his eyes over the varied assortment.

"How could he? The watches he might, but the other things. Why bless me, here are two pairs of earrings—and these grand pendants—I'm sure I saw them in the ears of the Condesa this very day. He couldn't have taken them without her knowing it. *Santo Dios!* How ever has he come by them?"

As he thus questioned and reflected, a feeling of apprehension began to creep over him. A little before leaving the house to go after his horses he had observed his young mistress and the Condesa going into the ornamental grounds. And they went alone; Don Ignacio having repaired to a private apartment, where he was accustomed to shut himself up for the examination of State papers, what if the ladies were still in the grounds, in some secluded spot, lying dead, where all these adornments had been stripped from their persons!

This horrible tableau did the faithful servant in imagination conjure up. He could not help it. Nor was the thing so very improbable. He had some earlier acquaintance with the desperate character of the dwarf, which later experience confirmed. Besides, there was the state of the country—thieves and robbers all round—men who made light of murder!

With a heaviness of heart—a painful fear that there had been murder—he stayed not to further examine the trinkets; but gathering all up again, and thrusting them back into his pocket, hurried on home.

And when home he went not to his own quarters in the coachyard, but straight into the *patio*—the private court of the house. There he encountered Pepita ; soon as he set eyes on her, asking—

" Where are the *Senoritas?* "

" What's that to you ? " saucily retorted the maid.

" Nothing, if I only knew they were safe."

" Safe ! Why what's the man thinking— talking about ? Have you lost your senses, *hombre?* "

" No, Pepita. But the ladies have lost something. Look here ! "

He had plunged both hands into his pockets, and drawn them out again full of things that scintillated in the moonlight— watches and jewellery of different kinds, as she saw. With a woman's curiosity, gliding swiftly forward to examine them, she recognised every article at a glance, amazement overspreading her countenance, as it lately had his.

" *A de mi !* " she exclaimed, no longer in jesting tone. " What does it all mean, José ? "

" Just what I want to know myself, and why I am asking after the Senoritas. But where are they ? "

" In the garden, or the grounds somewhere. They strolled out about an hour ago, and haven't been in since."

" Pray God, they're still alive ! Come with me, Pepita. Let us look for them. I have terrible fears."

So appealed to, the girl gave ready assent ; and side by side they hastened towards the rear of the house, behind which were the

ornamental grounds extending backwards.
But they had not far to go before hearing
sounds that set their minds at rest, removing
all anxiety—the voices of the ladies themselves. They were not only alive, but
laughing!

To José and Pepita this seemed strange as
anything else—a perfect mystery. Merry
after parting with all those pretty things;
costly, too—worth hundreds of *Doblones*!
Withal, they were so; their lightness of
heart due to the knowledge thus gained,
that their own lovers were still living and
safe; and something of merriment, added
by that odd encounter with the *enano*, of
which they were yet conversing.

If their behaviour mystified their servants,
not less were they themselves puzzled, when
José presented himself before them with
hands held out, saying:

"I ask your pardon for intruding, but don't these belong to your ladyships?"

They saw their watches and other effects obtained from them by "false pretences," as they were now to learn.

The revelation that succeeded put an end to their joyous humour; their hearts that had been light for a moment were now becoming heavier than ever. The treachery of the hunchback and his intentions were manifest. He meant to guide Santander and his soldiers to the old monastery where they would take the *patriotas* by surprise.

"What is to be done, Ysabel?" despairingly asked the Donna Luisa. "How can we give them warning?"

To which the *cochero*, not the Countess, made answer, saying:

"I can do that, *Senorita.*"

His confident tone reassured them; more

still his making known the design he had already conceived, and his ability to execute it. He was acquainted with the old convent and the paths leading to it—every inch of them.

It needed not their united appeal to urge him to immediate departure. He was off the instant after, and long before the clock of Talpam had struck the midnight hour well up the mountain road with eyes looking to the right, in the direction of the Cerro Ajusço.

## Chapter LIV.

## MONKS NO MORE.

THE surmise which had influenced Zorillo to leaving the convent cell earlier than he intended was a correct one. The goings on in the Refectory were, at the time, of an unusual kind—a grand occasion, as he had worded it. There were some fifty men in it; but not one of them now affecting either the garb or the behaviour of the monk. Soldiers all; or

at least in warlike guise; a few wearing
regular though undress uniforms, but the
majority habited as "guerilleros," in the
picturesque costumes of their country. They
were booted, and belted, swords by their
sides, with pistols in holsters hanging against
the walls, and spurs ready for buckling on.
Standing in corners were stacks of carbines,
and lances freshly pennoned, with their blades
bright from being recently sharpened—a
panoply which spoke of fighting ere long
expected to take place.

It may be asked, where were their horses,
since all the arms and accoutrements seen
around were those of cavalry? But horses
they had, though not there. Each knew
where to lay hands on his own, far or near,
stalled in the stable of some sequestered
*rancho*, or it might be mountain cavern.
They were not yet assembled to hearken to

the call of " Boot and Saddle ". That they
would hear at a later hour, and in a different
place.

The occasion of their being in such guise
and together, was because it was to be the
last night of their sojourn in the monastery.
And they were making it a merry one ; the
Refectory table was being loaded with the
best that was left to them in meats and
drinks. Upon it were what bottles remained
of those famous wines from the bins of the
rich *haciendado*—his forced contribution—
and they were fast getting emptied. From
the way the *convives* were quaffing, it was
not likely that any of the Burgundy, Madeira,
or Pedro Ximenes would be left behind—not
even a " heel-tap ".

It had got to be midnight, and they were
still in the midst of the revelry, when Rivas,
who headed the table, rose to his feet, in

that formal manner which tells of speech to be made or toast proclaimed.

"*Camaradas!*" he said, as soon as the buzz of conversation had ended, "As you're aware, we part from this place to-night; and some of you know whither we are going, and for what purpose. But not all; therefore I deem it my duty to tell you. You saw a courier who came up early this morning—bringing good news, I'm glad to say. This despatch I hold in my hand is from an old friend, General Alvarez; who, though he may not boast *sangre-azul* in his veins, is as brave a soldier, and pure a patriot, as any in the land. You know that. He tells me his *Pintos* are ready for a rising, and only wait for us—the "Free Lances"—with some others he has summoned to join him in giving the *grito*. By his messenger I have sent answer that we, too, are ready, and will respond to

his summons.    You all approve of that, I
take it ? "

"All !" was the exclaim in chorus, without
a dissenting voice.

"Moreover," proceeded the speaker, "I've
told the General we'll be on the march to-
morrow morning, and can meet him at a
place he has mentioned the day after.    His
plan is to attack the town of Oaxaca ; and, if
we succeed in taking it, then we move direct
on the capital.

"Now, *camarados*;  I've nothing more to
say ; only that you're to scatter after your
horses,  and  lose  no  time  in  mustering
again—the  old  rendezvous,  this  side  La
Guarda."

So ended the speech of the Free Lances'
leader, but despite the suggestions of immediate departure, the circle around the table
did not instantly break up.

The bottles were not all empty as yet, nor the revellers satisfied to leave them till they should be so. Besides, there was no particular need of haste for another hour or two. So they stuck to the table, smoking, drinking, and toasting many things, as persons, among the latter their lately joined allies —the *Irlandes* and *Tejano*, about whose proved valour on other fields, of which they had heard, the Free Lances were enthusiastically eloquent.

Kearney, speaking in their own tongue, made appropriate response ; while Rock, when told he had been toasted, delivered himself in characteristic strain, saying :—

" Feller-citizens,—For since I tuk up yur cause, I reck'n you'll gi'e me leave to call ye so—it air a glad thing to this chile to think he'll soon hev a bit o' fightin'. An' 'specially as its to be agin ole Santy, the durned

skunk. By the jumpin' Geehosofat! if Cris
Rock iver gits longside him agin, as he war
on't San Jacinty, there wan't be no more
meercy for the cussed tyrant, same as, like
a set of fools, we Texans showed him thar
an' then. Tell them what I sayed, Cap."

With which abrupt wind-up he dropped
back upon his seat, gulping down a tum-
blerful of best Madeira, as though it were
table-beer.

Kearney did tell them, translating his
comrade's speech faithfully as the *patois*
would permit; which heightened their en-
thusiasm, many of them starting to their
feet, rushing round the table, and, Mexican
fashion, enfolding the *Tejano* in friendly
embrace.

The hugging at an end, there was yet
another toast to follow, the same which always wound up the festivals of the "Free

Lances," whatever the occasion. Their leader, as often before, now again pronounced it—

"*Patria y Libertad!*"

And never before did it have more enthusiastic reception, the cheer that rang through the old convent, louder than any laughter of monks who may have ever made it their home.

Ere it had ceased reverberating, the door of the refectory was suddenly pushed open, and a man rushed into the room, as he entered, crying out—

"*Traicion!*"

"Treason!" echoed fifty voices as one, all again starting to their feet, and turning faces toward the alarmist. The mayor-domo it was, who, as the other *mozos*, was half equipped for a journey.

"What mean you, Gregorio?" demanded his master.

"There's one can tell you better than I, Don Ruperto."

"Who? Where is he?"

"Outside, Señor. A messenger who has just come up—he's from San Augustin."

"But how has he passed our sentry."

"Ah! *capitano;* I'd rather he told you himself."

Mysterious speech on the part of the mayor-domo, which heightened the apprehension of those hearing it.

"Call him hither!" commanded Rivas.

No calling was needed; the person spoken of being in the environ close by; and Gregorio, again opening the door, drew him inside.

The *cochero!* mentally exclaimed Rivas, Kearney, and the Texan, soon as setting eyes on him.

The *cochero* it was, José, though they

knew not his name nor anything more of him than what they had learned in that note of the Condesa's saying that he could be trusted, and their brief association with him afterwards—which gave them proof that he could.

As he presented himself inside the room he seemed panting for breath, and really was. He had only just arrived up the steep climb, and exchanged hardly half a dozen words with the mayor-domo, who had met him at the outside entrance.

Announced as a messenger, neither the Captain of the Free Lances nor Florence Kearney needed telling who sent him. A sweet intuition told them that. Rivas but asked,

"How have you found the way up here?"

"*Por Dios! Señor*, I've been here before— many's the time. I was born among these mountains—am well acquainted with all the paths everywhere around."

" But the sentry below. How did you get past him ?  You haven't the countersign !"

" He wouldn't have heard it if I had, Señor. Pobre ! he'll never hear countersign again— nor anything else."

" Why ?  Explain yourself !"

" *Esta muerto !* He's lies at the bottom of the cliff his body crushed—"

" Who has done it ?  Who's betrayed us ?" interrupted a volley of voices.

" The hunchback, Zorillo," answered José, to the astonishment of all.  For in the dialogue between the dwarf and Santander, he had heard enough to anticipate the ghastly spectacle awaiting him on his way up the mountain.

Cries of anger and vengeance were simultaneously sent up ; all showing eager to rush from the room. They but waited for a word more.

Rivas, however, suspecting that the messenger meant that word for himself, claimed their indulgence, and led him outside, inviting Kearney to accompany them.

Though covering much ground, and relating to many incidents, the *cochero's* story was quickly told. Not in the exact order of occurrence, but as questioned by his impatient listeners. He ran rapidly over all that happened, since their parting at the corner of the Coyoacan road, the latter events most interesting them. Surprised were they to hear that Don Ignacio and his daughter for some time had been staying at San Augustin—the Condesa with them. Had they but known that before, in all probability things would not have been as now. Possibly they might have been worse; though, even as they stood, there was enough danger impending over all. As for themselves, both Mexican and Irishman, less recked of it, as they thought of how they were being warned, and by whom. That of itself was recompense for all their perils.

Meanwhile, those left inside the room were chafing to learn the particulars of the treason, though they were not all there now. Some had sallied out, and gone down the cliff to bring up the body of their murdered comrade ; others, the mayor-domo conducting, back to the place where the hunchback should be, but was not. There to find confirmation of what had been said. The cell untenanted ; the window bar filed through and broken ; the file lying by it, and the chain hanging down outside.

Intelligible to them now was the tale of treason, without their hearing it told.

When once more they assembled in the

Refectory, it was with chastened, saddened hearts. For they had come from digging a grave, and lowering into it a corpse. Again gathered around the table they drank the stirrup-cup, as was their wont, but never so joylessly, or with such stinted acclaim.

## Chapter LV.

### "ONLY EMPTY BOTTLES."

BOUT the time the Free Lances were burying their comrade in the cemetery of the convent, the gate of San Antonio de Abad was opened to permit the passage of a squadron of Hussars going outward from the city. There were nigh 200 of them, in formation "by fours" —the wide causeway allowing ample room for even ten abreast.

At their head rode Colonel Santander, with Major Ramirez by his side, other officers in their places distributed along the line.

Soon as they had cleared the *garita*, a word to the bugler, with a note or two from his trumpet quick succeeding, set them into a gallop; the white dusty road and clear moonlight making the fastest pace easily attainable. And he who commanded was in haste, his destination being that old monastery, of which he had only lately heard, but enough to make him most eager to reach it before morning. His hopes were high; at last was he likely to make a *coup* — that capture so much desired, so long delayed!

For nearly an hour bridles were let loose, and spurs repeatedly plied. On along the *calzada* swept the squadron, over the bridge Churubusco, and past the hacienda of San Antonio de Abad, which gives its name to

the city gate on that side. Thenceforward
the Pedregal impinges on the road, and the
Hussars still going at a gallop along its
edge, another bugle-call brought them to a
halt.

That, however, had naught to do with their
halting, which came from their commander,
having reached the spot where he had left
the hunchback in charge of the two
soldiers.

He need not hailing them to assure himself they were still there. The trampling of
horses on the hard causeway, heard afar off,
had long ago forewarned the corporal of
what was coming ; and he was out on the
road to receive them, standing in an attitude of attention.

The parley was brief, and quick the action
which accompanied it.

" Into your saddle, *cabo !* " commanded the

colonel. "Take that curiosity up behind you and bring it along."

In an instant the corporal was mounted, the "curiosity" hoisted up to his croup by Perico, who then sprang to the back of his own horse. Once more the bugle gave tongue, and away they went again.

The cavalcade made no stop in San Augustin. There was no object for halting it there, and delay was the thing its commander most desired to avoid. As they went clattering through the *pueblo* its people were a-bed, seemingly asleep. But not all. Two at least were awake, and heard that unusual noise— listened to it with a trembling in their frames and fear in their hearts. Two ladies they were, inside a house beyond the village, on the road running south. Too well knew they what it meant, and whither the galloping cohort was bound. And themselves unseen, they saw who was at the head; though they needed not seeing him to know. But peering through the *jalousies*, the moonlight revealed to them the face of Don Carlos Santander, in the glimpse they got of it, showing spitefully triumphant.

He could not see them, though his eyes interrogated the windows while he was riding past. They had taken care to extinguish the light in their room.

"*Virgin Santissima!* Mother of God!" exclaimed one of the ladies, Luisa Valverde, as she dropped on her knees in prayer, "Send that they've got safe off ere this!"

"Make your mind easy, *amiga!*" counselled the Condesa Almonté in less precatory tone. "I'm good as sure they have. José cannot fail to have reached and given them warning. That will be enough."

A mile or so beyond San Augustin the

southern road becomes too steep for horses to go at a gallop, without risk of breaking their wind. So there the Hussars had to change to a slower pace—a walk in fact. There were other reasons for coming to this. The sound of their hoof-strokes ascending would be heard far up the mountain, might reach the ears of those in the monastery, and so thwart the surprise intended for them.

While toiling more leisurely up the steep, any one chancing to look in the hunchback's face would there have observed an expression indescribable. Sadness pervaded it, with an air of perplexity, as though he had met with some misfortune he could not quite comprehend.

And so had he. Before leaving the spot where the stiletto was taken from him, he had sought an opportunity to step back into that shady niche in the cliff where he had lost his treasures. The *monté* players, unsuspicious of his object, made no objection. But instead of there finding what he expected, he saw only a pair of horse-halters : one lying coiled upon the ground, the head-stall of the other caught over the rock above, the rope end dangling down !

An inexplicable phenomenon which, however, he had kept to himself, and ever since been cudgelling his brains to account for.

But soon after he had something else to think of ; the time having arrived when he was called upon to give proof of his capability as a guide. Heretofore it had been all plain road riding ; but now they had reached a point spoken of by himself, where the *calzada* must be forsaken. The horses, too, left behind ; everything but their weapons ; the path beyond being barely practicable for men afoot.

Dismounting all, at a command—this time not given by the bugle—and leaving a sufficient detail to look after the animals, they commenced the ascent, their guide, seemingly more quadruped than biped, in the lead. Strung out in single file—no other formation being possible—as they wound their way up the zig-zag with the moonlight here and there, giving back the glint of their armour, it was as some great serpent —a monster of the antediluvian ages—crawling towards its prey. Silently as serpent too ; not a word spoken, nor exclamation uttered along their line. For, although it might be another hour before they could reach their destination, less than a second would suffice for their voices to get there, even though but muttered.

One spot their guide passed with something like a shudder. It was where he had appropriated the dagger taken from a dead body. His shuddering was not due to that, but to fear from a far different cause. The body was no longer there. Those who dwelt above must have been down and borne it away. They would now be on the alert, and at any moment he might hear the cracking of carbines—a volley; perhaps feel the avenging bullet! What if they should roll rocks down and crush him and the party behind? In any case there could be no surprisal now; and he would gladly have seen those he was guiding give up the thought of it and turn back. Santander was himself irresolute, and would willingly have done so. But Ramirez, a man of more mettle, at the point of his sword commanded the hunchback to keep on, and the cowardly colonel dare not revoke the order without eternally disgracing himself.

They had no danger to encounter, though they knew not that. Neither vidette nor sentinel was stationed there now; and, without challenge or obstruction, they reached the platform on which the building stood, the soldiers taking to right and left till they swarmed around it as bees. But they found no honey inside that hive.

There was a summons to surrender, which received no response. Repeated louder, and a carbine fired, the result was the same. Silence inside, there could be no one within.

Nor was there. When the Hussar colonel, with a dozen of his men, at length screwed up courage to make a burst into the doorway, and on to the refectory, they saw but the evidence of late occupancy in the fragments of a supper, with some dozens of wine bottles "down among the dead men," empty as the building itself.

Disappointed as were the soldiers at finding them so, but still more their commanding officer at his hated enemies having again got away from him. His soul was brimful of chagrin, nor did it allay the feeling to learn how, when a path was pointed out to him leading down the other side, they must have made off. And along such a path pursuit was idle. No one could say where it led—like enough to a trap.

He was not the only one of the party who felt disappointed at the failure of the expedition. Its guide had reason to be chagrined, too, in his own way of thinking, much more than the leader himself. For not only had he lost the goods obtained under false pretences, but the hope of reward for his volunteered services.

Still the dwarf was not so down in the mouth. He had another arrow in his quiver

—kept in reserve for reasons of his own—
a shaft from which he expected more profit
than all yet spent. And as the Hussar colonel
was swearing and raging around, he saw his
opportunity to discharge it. With half a
dozen whispered words he tranquillised the
latter; after which there was a brief confer-
ence between the two, its effect upon Santander showing itself in his countenance, that
became all agleam, lit up with a satisfied but
maligant joy.

When, in an hour after, they were again
in their saddles riding in return for the City,
a snatch of dialogue between Santander and
Ramirez gave indication of what so gratified
the colonel of Hussars.

" Well, Major," he said " we've done road
enough for this day. You'll be wanting rest
by the time you get to quarters."

" That's true enough, Colonel. Twice to

San Augustin and back, with the additional mileage up the mountains—twenty leagues, I take it—to say nothing of the climbing."

"All of twenty leagues it will be, when we've done with it. But our ride won't be over then. If I'm not mistaken, we'll be back this way before we lay side on a bed. There's another nest not far off will claim a visit from us, one we're not likely to find so empty. I'd rob it now if I had my way; but, for certain reasons, mus'nt without permit from Head-Quarters; the which I'm sure of getting! *Carajo!* if the cock birds have escaped, I'll take care the hens don't."

And as if to make sure of it he dug the spurs deep into the flanks of his now jaded charger, again commanding the "quick gallop".

## Chapter LVI.

## A DAY OF SUSPENSE.

DAWN was just beginning to show over the eastern *Cordilleras*, its aurora giving a rose tint to the snowy cone of Popocatepec, as the Hussars passed back through San Augustin. The bells of the *paroquia* had commenced tolling matins and many people abroad in the streets, hurrying toward the church, saw them—interrogating one another, as to where they had been, and on what errand bound.

But before entering the *pueblo*, they had to
pass under the same eyes that observed them
going outward on the other side ; these more
keenly and anxiously scrutinising them now,
noting every file as it came in sight, every
individual horseman, till the last was revealed;
then lighting up with joyous sparkle, while
they thus observing, breathed freely.

For the soldiers had come as they went ; not
a man added to their number, if none missing;
but certainly no prisoners brought back !

" They've got safe off," triumphantly exclaimed the Countess, when the rearmost files
had forged past, " as I told you they would ;
I knew there was no fear after they had been
warned."

That they had been warned both were by
this aware ; their messenger having meanwhile
returned and reported to that effect.   He had
met the Hussars on their way up ; but crouch-

ing among some bushes, he had been unobserved by them ; and, soon as they were well
out of the way, slipped out again and made all
haste home.

He had brought back something more than
a mere verbal message—a *billetita* for each of
the two who had commissioned him.

The notes were alike, in that both had been
hastily scribbled, and in brief but warm expression of thanks for the service done to the
writers.   Beyond this, however, they were
quite different.   It was the first epistle
Florence Kearney had ever indited to Louisa
Valverde, and ran in fervid strain.   He felt he
could so address her.   With love long in doubt
that it was even reciprocated, but sure of its
being so now, he spoke frankly, as passion-
ately.   Whatever his future, she had his heart,
and wholly.   If he lived he would seek her
again at the peril of a thousand lives ; if it

should be his fate to die, her name would be
the last word on his lips.

" *Virgen Santissima!*    Keep him safe ! "
was her prayer, as she finished devouring
the sweet words ; then, refolding the sheet
on which they were written, secreted it away
in the bosom of her dress—a treasure more
esteemed than aught that had ever lain
there.

The communication received by the Condesa was less effusive, and more to the point
of what, under present circumstances, concerned the writer—as, indeed, all of them.
Don Ruperto wrote with the confidence of
a lover who had never known doubt.   A man
of rare qualities, he was true to friendship
as to his country's cause, and would not be
false to love.   And he had no fear of her.
His *liens* with Ysabel Almonté were such as
to preclude all thought of her affections ever

changing. He knew that she was his—
heart, soul, everything. For had she not
given him every earnest of it—befriended
him through weal and through woe? Nor
had he need to assure her that her love was
reciprocated, or his fealty still unfaltering;
for their faith, as their reliance, was mutual.
His letter, therefore, was less that of a lover
to his mistress, than one between man and
man, written to a fellow-conspirator; most
of it in figurative phrase, even some of it
in cypher !

No surprise to her all that; she understood the reason. Nor was there any enigma
in the signs and words of double significa-
cation; without difficulty she interpreted
them all.

They told her of the anticipated rising,
with the attempt to be made on Oaxaca;
the hopes of its having a success; and, if so,

what would come after. But also of something before this where he, the writer, and
his Free Lances would be on the following
night, so that if need arose she could communicate with him. If she had apprehension
of danger to him, he was not without
thought of the same threatening herself, and
her friend too.

Neither were they now ; instead, filled
with such apprehension. In view of what
had occurred on the preceding evening, and
throughout the night, how could they be
other ? The dwarf must know more than
he had revealed in that dialogue overheard
by José. In short, he seemed aware of
everything—the *cochero's* complicity, as their
own. The free surrender of their watches
and jewellery for the support of the escaped
prisoners were of itself enough to incriminate
them. Surely would there be another inves-

tigation, more rigorous than before, and likely to have a different ending.

With this in contemplation, their souls full of fear, neither went that morning to matins. Nor did they essay to take sleep or rest. Instead, wandered about the house from room to room, and out into the grounds seemingly distraught.

They had the place all to themselves; no one to take counsel with, none to comfort them; Don Ignacio, at an early hour, having been called off to his duties in the city. But they were not destined to spend the whole of that day without seeing a visitor. As the clocks of San Augustin were striking 8 p.m. one presented himself at the gate, in the guise of an officer of Hussars—Don Carlos Santander. Nor was he alone, but with an escort accompanying. They were seated in the verandah of the inner court, but saw him through the *saguan*, the door of which was open ; saw him enter at the outer gate, and without dismounting come on towards them, several files of his men following. He had been accustomed to visit them there, and they to receive his visits, however reluctantly ; reasons of many kinds compelling them. But never had he presented himself as now. It was an act of ill-manners his entering unannounced ; another riding into the enclosure with soldiers behind him ; but the rudeness was complete when he came on into the *patio* still in the saddle—his men, too—and pulled up directly in front of them, without waiting for word of invitation. The stiff formal bow ; the expression upon his swarthy features, severe, but with ill-concealed exultation in it, proclaimed his visit of no complimentary kind.

By this both were on their feet, looking

offended—even angry—at the same time alarmed. And yet little surprised; for it was only confirmation of the fear that had been all day oppressing them—its very fulfilment. But that they believed it this, they would have shown their resentment by retiring and leaving him there. As it was, they knew that would be idle, and so stayed to hear what he had to say. It was—

"*Senoritas*, I see you're wondering at my thus presenting myself. Not strange you should. Nor could anyone more regret the disagreeable errand I've come upon than I. It grieves me sorely, I assure you."

"What is it, Colonel Santander?" demanded the Countess, with *sang-froid* partially restored.

"I hate to declare it, Condesa," he rejoined; "still more to execute it. But compelled by the rigorous necessities of a soldier's duty, I must.

" Well, sir ; must what ? "

" Make you a prisoner ; and, I am sorry to add, also the Dona Luisa."

" Oh, that's it ! " exclaimed the Countess, with a scornful inclination of the head. " Well, sir, I don't wonder at your disliking the duty, as you say you do. It seems more that of a policeman than a soldier."

The retort struck home, still further humiliating him in the eyes of the woman he loved, Luisa Valverde. But he now knew she loved not him; and had made up his mind to humble her, in a way hitherto untried. Stung by the innuendo, and dropping his clumsy pretence at politeness, he spitefully rejoined :—

"Thank you, Condesa Almonté, for your amiable observation. It does something to compensate me for having to do policeman's duty. And now let it be done. Please to consider yourself under arrest; and you also, Senorita Valverde."

Up to this time the last-named lady had not said a word; the distress she was in restraining her. But as mistress there, she saw it was her turn to speak, which she did, saying :—

"If we are your prisoners, Colonel Santander, I hope you will not take us away from here till my father comes home. As you may be aware, he's in the city."

"I am aware of that, Dona Luisa; and glad to say my orders enable me to comply with your wishes, and that you remain here till Don Ignacio returns. I'm enjoined to see to your safe keeping. A very absurd requirement, but one which often falls to the lot of the soldier as well as the *policeman*."

Neither the significant words nor the forced laugh that accompanied them had any effect on her for whom they were intended. With disdain in her eyes, such as a captive queen might show for the common soldier who stood guard over her, the Condesa had already turned her back upon the speaker and was walking away. With like proud air, but less confident and scornful, Luisa Valverde followed. Both were allowed to pass inside, leaving the Hussar colonel to take such measures for their keeping as he might think fit.

His first step was to order in the remainder of his escort and distribute them around the house; so that in ten minutes after the *casa de campo* of Don Ignacio Valverde bore resemblance to a barrack, with sentinels at every entrance and corner!

## Chaptrr LVII.

### UNDER ARREST.

SCARCE necessary to say that Luisa Valverde and Ysabel Almonté were at length really alarmed—fully alive to a sense of their danger.

It was no more a question of the safety of their lovers, but their own. And the prospect was dark, indeed. Santander had said nothing of the reason for arresting them; nor had they cared to inquire. They divined it ; no longer doubting that it was owing to revelations made by the hunchback.

Sure now that this diminutive wretch not only himself knew their secret, but had made it known in higher quarters, there seemed no hope for them ; instead, ruin staring them in the face. The indignity to their persons they were already experiencing, would be followed by social disgrace, and confiscation of property.

" O, Ysabelita ! what will they do to us ? " was the Dona Luisa's anxious interrogatory, soon as they had got well inside their room. " Do you think they'll put us in a prison ? "

" Possibly they will. I wish there was nothing worse awaiting us."

" Worse ! Do you mean they'd inflict punishment on us—that is, corporal punishment ? Surely they daren't ? "

" Daren't ! Santa Anna dare anything—

at least, neither shame nor mercy will restrain him. No more this other man, his minion, whom you know better than I. But it isn't punishment of that kind I'm thinking of."

"What then, Ysabel? The loss of our property? It'll be all taken from us, I suppose."

"In all likelihood it will," rejoined the Condesa, with as much unconcern as though her estates, value for more than a million, were not worth a thought.

"Oh! my poor father! This new misfortune, and all owing to me. 'Twill kill him!"

"No, no, Lusita! Don't fear that. He will survive it, if aught survives of our country's liberty. And it will, all of it, be restored again. 'Tis something else I was thinking of."

Again the other asked "What?" her countenance showing increased anxiety.

"What we as women have more to fear than aught else. From the loss of lands, houses, riches of any sort, one may recover—from the loss of that, never?"

Enigmatic as were the words, Luisa Valverde needed no explanation of them; nor pressed for it. She comprehended all now, and signified her apprehension by exclaiming, with a shudder. "*Virgen Santissima!*"

"The prison they will take us to," pursued the Countess, "is a place—that in the Plaza Grande. We shall be immured there, and at the mercy of that man, that monster! O God!—O Mother of God, protect me!"

At which she dropped down upon a couch, despairingly, with face buried in her hands.

It was a rare thing for the Condesa Almonté to be so moved—rather to show despondence —and her friend was affected accordingly.

For there was another man at whose mercy she herself would be—one like a monster, and as she well knew equally unmerciful— he who at that moment was under the same roof with them—in her father's house, for the time its master.

"But, Ysabel," she said, hoping against hope, "surely they will not dare to——"

She left the word unspoken, knowing it was not needed to make her meaning understood.

"Not dare!" echoed the Countess, recovering nerve and again rising to her feet. "As I've said he'll dare anything—will Don Antonio Lopes de Santa Anna. Besides, what has *he* to fear? Nothing. He can show good cause for our imprisonment else he would never have had us arrested. Enough to satisfy any clamour of the people. And how would any one ever know of what might be done to us inside the Palacio? Ah, *Lusita querida;* if its walls could speak they might tell tales sad enough to make angels weep. We would'nt be the first who have been subjected to insult—ay, infamy—by *El excellentissimo. Vaga me Dios!*" she cried out in conclusion, stamping her foot on the floor, while the flash of her eyes told of some fixed determination. "If it be so, that Palace prison will have another secret to keep, or a tale to tell, sad and tragic as any that has preceded. I, Ysabel Almonté, shall die in it rather than come out dishonoured."

"I, too!" echoed Luisa Valverde, if in less excited manner, inspired by a like heroic resolve.

\* \* \* \* \* \* \* \*

While his fair prisoners were thus exchanging thought and speech, Santander, in the *sala grande* outside, was doing his best to pass the time pleasantly. An effort it was costing him, however, and one far from successful. His last lingering hope of being beloved by Luisa Valverde was gone—completely destroyed by what had late come to his knowledge—and henceforth his love for her could only be as that of Tarquin for Lucretia. Nor would he have any Collatinus to fear—no rival, martial or otherwise—since his master, Santa Anna, had long since given up his designs on Don Ignacio's daughter; exclusively bending himself to his scheme of conquest—now revenge—over the Condesa. But though relieved in this regard, and likely to have his own way, Carlos Santander was anything but a happy man after making that arrest; instead, almost as miserable as either of those he had arrested.

Still keeping up a pretence of gallantry, he could not command their company in the

drawing-room where he had installed himself;
nor, under the circumstances, would it have
been desirable. He was not alone, however;
Major Ramirez and the other officers of his
escort being there with him; and, as in like
cases, they were enjoying themselves. However considerate for the feelings of the ladies,
they made free enough with the house itself,
its domestics, larder, and *cocina*, and, above
all, the cellar. Its binns were inquired into,
the best wine ordered to be brought from
them, as though they who gave the order
were the guests of an hotel, and Don Ignacio's
drawing-room a drinking saloon.

Outside in the court-yard, and further off
by the coach-house, similar scenes were trans-
piring. Never had that quiet *casa de
campo* known so much noise. For the
soldiers had got among them—it was the house
of a *rebel*, and therefore devoted to ruin.

## Chapter LVIII.

### THE COCHERO DOGGED.

UST after the ladies had been pro-claimed under arrest, but before the the sentinels were posted around the house, a man might have been seen out-side their line, making all haste away from it. He had need, his capture being also contem-plated. José it was, who, from a place of concealment, had not only seen what passed, but heard the conversation between Santander

and the Señoritas. The words spoken by his
young mistress, and the rejoinder received,
were all he waited for. Giving him his cue
for departure, they also gave him hopes of
something more than the saving of his own
life. That the last was endangered he knew
now—forfeited indeed, should he fall into the
hands of those who had invaded the place.
So instead of returning to the stable yard,
from which he had issued on hearing the
*fracas* in front, he retreated rearwards, first
through the ornamental grounds, then over
the wall upon which the hunchback had
perched himself on the preceding night. José,
however, did not stay on it for more than a
second's time. Soon as mounting to its
summit, he slid down on the other side, and
ran along the lane in the direction of the
main road.

Before reaching this, however, a reflection

caused him to slacken pace, and then come to a stop. It was still daylight, and there would be a guard stationed by the front gate, sure to see him along the road. The ground on the opposite side of the lane was a patch of rocky scrub—in short a *chapparal*—into which in an instant after he plunged, and when well under cover again made stop; this time dropping down on his hands and knees. The attitude gave him a better opportunity of listening; and listen he did—all ears.

To hear voices all around the house, loudest in the direction of the stable yard. In tones not of triumph, but telling of disappointment. For in truth it was so; the shouts of the soldiers searching for his very self, and swearing because he could not be found. He had reason to congratulate himself in having got outside the enclosure. It was now being quartered everywhere, gardens, grounds and all.

For the time he felt comparatively safe; but he dared not return to the lane. And less show himself on the open road; as scouting parties were sure of being sent out after him. There was no alternative, therefore, but stay where he was till the darkness came down. Luckily, he would not have long to wait for it. The sun had set, and twilight in the Mexican valley is but a brief interval between day and night. In a few minutes after commencement, it is over.

Short as it was it gave him time to consider his future course of action, though that required little consideration. It had been already traced out for him, partly by the Condesa, in an interview he held with her but an hour before, and partly by instructions he had received when up at the old convent direct from the lips of Don Ruperto. Therefore, hurried as was his retreat, he was not

making it as one who went blindly, and
without definite aim. He had this, with a
point to be reached; which, could he only
arrive at, not only might his own safety be
secured, but that of those he was equally
anxious about, now more imperilled than
himself.

With a full comprehension of their danger,
and the hope of being able to avert it, soón
as the twilight deepened to darkness, he
forsook his temporary place of concealment;
and, returning to the lane, glided noiselessly
along it towards the main road. Coming
out upon this, he turned to the left, and
without looking behind, hurried up the hill
as fast as his limbs could carry him.

Perhaps better for him had he looked behind; and yet in the end it might have
been worse. Whether or no, he was followed
by a man—if it were a man—and, if a thing,

not his own shadow. A grotesque creature, seemingly all arms and legs, moved after, keeping pace with him, no matter how rapidly he progressed. Not overtaking him ; though it looked as if able to do so, but did not wish. Just so it was—the stalker being Zorilla.

The stalk had risen rather accidentally. The hunchback—now in a manner attached to the party of Hussars—had been himself loitering near the end of the lane, and saw the *cochero* as he came out on the road. He knew the latter was being sought for, and by no one more zealously than himself. Besides cupidity, he was prompted by burning revenge. The disappearance of his ill-gotten treasure was no longer a mystery to him. The abandoned halters, with the horses for which they had been intended, told him all. Only the *cochero* could have carried the things off.

And now, seeing the latter as he stole away in retreat, his first impulse was to raise the hue and cry, and set the soldiers after. But other reflections, quick succeeding, restrained him. They might not be in time to secure a capture. In the darkness there was every chance of the *mertizo* eluding them. A tract of forest was not far off, and he would be into it before they could come up. Besides, the hunchback had also conjectured that the failure of their overnight expedition was due to José. He must have overheard that conversation with the colonel of Hussars, and carried it direct to those whom it so seriously concerned, thus saving them from the surprise intended. In all likelihood he was now on his way to another interview with them.

If so, and if he, Zorilla, could but spot the place, and bring back report of it to

Santander, it would give him a new claim for services, and some compensation for the loss he had sustained through the now hated *cochero*.

Soon as resolved, he lost not a moment in making after, keeping just such distance between as to hinder José from observing him. He had the advantage in being behind; as it was all uphill, and from below he could see the other by the better light above, while himself in obscurity. But he also availed himself of the turnings of the road, and the scrub that grew alongside it, through which he now and then made way. His long legs gave a wonderful power of speed, and he could have come up with the *mertizo* at any moment. He knew that, but knew also it would likely cost him his life. For the *cochero* must be aware of what he had done— enough to deserve death at his hands. He might well dread an encounter, and was careful to avoid it. Indeed, but for his belief that he was an overmatch for the other in speed he would not have ventured after him.

For nearly five miles up the mountain road the stalk was continued. Then he, whose footsteps were so persistently dogged, was seen to turn into a side path, which led along a ravine still upward. But the change, of course, did not throw off the sleuth-hound skulking on his track, the latter also entering the gorge, and gliding on after.

There it was darker, from the shadow of the overhanging cliffs; and for a time the hunchback lost sight of him he was following. Still he kept on, groping his way, and at length was rewarded by seeing a light—a great blaze. It came from a bivouac fire, which threw its red glare on the rocks around,

embracing within its circle the forms of men
and horses. Armed men they were, and
horses caparisoned for war; as could be told
by the glint of weapons and accoutrements
given back to the fire's blaze.

There appeared·to be over a hundred of
them; but the hunchback did not approach
near enough to make estimate of their number. Enough for him to know who they
were; and this knowledge he obtained by
seeing a man of gigantic size standing by
the side of the fire—the " big *Tejano!* "
He saw, too, that the *cochero* had got upon
the ground, his arrival creating an excite-
ment. But he stayed to see no more: his
purpose was fulfilled; and turning back
down the ravine, he again got out to the
road, where he put on his best speed in return for Tlalpam.

## Chapter LIX.

### READY TO START.

S in all Mexican country houses of the class mansion, that of Don Ignacio Valverde was a quadrangular structure enclosing an inner court-yard—the *patio*. The latter a wide open area, flagged, in its centre a playing fountain, with orange trees and other ornamental evergreens growing in great boxes around it. Along three sides ran a verandah gallery, raised a step or two above the pavement, with a baluster and railing between. Upon this opened the doors of the different chambers, as they would into the hall-way of an English house. Being one-storeyed, even the sleeping apartments were entered direct from it.

That into which the ladies had retired was the *cuarto de camara* of Don Luisa herself. No sentry had been stationed at its door; this being unnecessary, in view of one posted at the entrance to the *patio*. But through a casement window, which opened into the garden at the back, they could see such precaution had been taken. A soldier out there, with carbine thrown lightly over his left arm, was doing his beat backwards and forwards.

As they had no thought of attempting escape, they might have laughed at this, had they been in a mood for merriment. But they were sad, even to utter prostration.

Only for a time, however; then something of hope seemed to reanimate the Condesa, and communicate itself to her companion. It was after a report brought in by Pepita; for the lady's maid was allowed to attend upon them, coming and going freely.

"He's got away—safe!" were her words, spoken in a cautious but cheering tone, as for the second time she came into the room.

"Are you sure, Pepita?"

It was the Countess who put the question.

"Quite sure, your ladyship. I've been all around the place, to the stable, grounds, everywhere, and couldn't hear or see anything of him. Oh! he's gone, and so glad I am. They'd have made him prisoner too. Thanks to the Blessed Virgin, they haven't."

The thanksgiving was for José, and however fervent on Pepita's part, it was as fervently responded to by the others, the Condesa seeming more especially pleased at the intelligence.

She better understood its importance, for, but the hour before, she had given him conditional instructions, and hoped he might be now in the act of carrying them out.

Upheld by this hope, which the Dona Luisa, when told of it shared with her, they less irksomely passed the hours.

But at length, alas! it, too, was near being given up, as the night grew later, nearing midnight. Then the little mertiza came in charged with new intelligence; not so startling, since they anticipated it. The *Dueno* had got home, and, as themselves, was under arrest. Astounded by what he had learned on return, and angrily protesting, the soldiers had rudely seized hold of him, even refusing him permission to speak with his daughter.

She had harboured a belief that all might be well on the coming home of her father. The last plank was shattered now. From the chair of the cabinet minister Don Ignacio Valverde would step direct into the cell of a prison! Nothing uncommon in the political history of Mexico—only one of its " cosas ".

On their feet they were now, and had come close to the door, which was held slightly open by Pepita. There they stood listening to what was going on outside. The sounds of revelry lately proceeding from the *sala grande* were no more heard. Instead, calls and words of command in the courtyard, with a bustle of preparation. Through the trellis-work they could see a carriage with horses attached, distinguishable as their own. It was the same which had just brought Don

Ignacio from the city. But the heads of the *frisones* were turned outward, as if it was intended to take them back. Men on horseback were moving around it; soldiers, as could be seen by their armour gleaming in the moonlight.

Those regarding their movements were not left long in suspense as to their meaning. One of the soldiers on foot, whose sleeve chevrons proclaimed him a corporal, stepped up into the corridor, and advancing along it, halted in front of their door. Seeing it open, with faces inside, he made a sort of military salute, in a gruff voice saying:

" *Senoritas!* Carriage ready. I've orders to conduct you to it without delay."

There was something offensive in the man's manner. He spoke with a thick tongue, and was evidently half intoxicated. But his air showed him in earnest.

" You'll allow us a little time—to put on our cloaks ? "

The request came from the Condesa, who for a certain reason was wishful to retard their departure as long as might be possible.

" *Carrai—i!* " drawled out the *cabo*, the same who had won the dagger from darling Perico. " I'd allow such beautiful doncellas as you any time—all night—if 'twere only left to me. For myself, I'd far rather stick to these snug quarters, and the company of of this pretty *muchacha*."

At which, leaning forward, with a brutish leer, he attempted to snatch a kiss from Pepita.

The girl shrunk back, but not till she had rebuked him with an angry retort and a slap across the cheek. It stung him to losing temper, and without further ceremony he said spitefully—

"Come, come, I'll have no more dilly-dallying ; *nos vamos !*"

There was no alternative but to obey ; his attitude told them he would insist upon it, and instantly. Time for cloaking had been a pretence on their part. They were expecting the summons, and the wraps were close at hand. Flinging them around their shoulders, and drawing the hoods over their heads, they issued out upon the corridor, and turned along it—the soldier preceding, with the air of one who conducted criminals to execution.

A short flight of steps led down to the pavement of the court. On reaching these, they paused and looked below. There was still a bustling about the carriage, as if some one had just been handed into it. Several of the soldiers were on foot around it, but the majority were in their saddles ; and of these three or four could be distinguished as officers by the greater profusion of gold lace on their jackets and dolmans—for they were all Hussars. One who glittered more than any, seeing them at the head of the stair, gave his horse a prick with the spur, and rode up. Colonel Santander it was, like all the rest somewhat excited by drink; but still not so far gone as to forget gallantry, or rather the pretence of it.

" Ladies," he said, with a bow and air of maudlin humility, " I have to apologise for requiring you to start out on a journey at such a late hour. Duty is often an ungracious master. Luckily, your drive is not to be a very extended one—only to the city; and you'll have company in the carriage. The Dona Luisa will find her father at home."

Neither vouchsafed rejoinder—not a word —scarce giving him the grace of a look.

Which a little nettling him, his smooth tone changed to asperity, as addressing himself to the soldier, he gave the abrupt order :

" *Cabo !* take them on to the carriage."

On they were taken ; as they approached it, perceiving a face inside, pale as the moonbeams that played upon it. It was a very picture of dejection ; for never had Don Ignacio Valverde experienced misery such as he felt now.

"'Tis you, father!" said his daughter, springing up, throwing her arms around him, and showering kisses, where tears already trickled. " You a prisoner too !"

" Aye, *nina mia*. But sit down. Don't be alarmed ! It will all come right. Heaven will have mercy on us, if men do not. Sit down, Luisa !"

She sat down mechanically, the Countess by her side ; and the door was banged to

behind them. Meanwhile, Pepita, who in-
sisted on accompanying her mistress, had
been handed up to the box by a *cochero*
strange to her; one of the soldiers, pressed
into the service for the occasion, a *quondam*
"jarvey," who understood the handling of
horses as every Mexican does.

All were now ready for the road; the dismounted Hussars had vaulted into théir
saddles, the "march" was commanded, and
the driver had drawn his whip to lay it on
his horses, when the animals jibbed, rearing
up, and snorting in affright!

No wonder; with such an object suddenly
coming under their eyes. An oddly-shaped
creature that came scrambling in through
the *saguan* and made stop beneath their
very noses. A human being withal; who,
soon as entering, called out, in a clear voice—

"Where is the Colonel?"

## Chapter LX.

### "SURRENDER!"

IF the carriage horses were startled by the apparition, no less so were the Hussars formed round. Equally frightened these, though not from the same cause. The hunchback—for it was he—had become a familiar sight to them; but not agitated as he appeared to be now. He was panting for breath, barely able to gasp out the interrogation, "Adone 'stael Coronel?"

His distraught air and the tone told of some threatening danger.

"Here!" called out Santander, springing his horse a length or two forward, "What is it, sirrah?"

"The enemy, S'ñor Coronel," responded the dwarf, sliding close in to the strirup

"Enemy! What enemy?"

"Them we missed catching—Don Ruperto, the Irlandes, the big Tejano."

"Ha!—They!—Where!"

"Close by. S'ñor. I saw them round a great camp fire up in the mountains. They're not there now. I came on to tell you. I ran as fast as ever I was able, but they've been following. I could hear the tramp of their horses behind all the way. They must be near at hand now. Hark!"

"Patriar y Libertad!"

The cry came from without, in the tone

of a charging shibboleth, other voices adding,
" Mueran los tyrannos ! " Instantaneously succeeded by the cracking of carbines, with
shouts, and the clash of steel against steel—
the sounds of a hand-to-hand fight, which
the stamping and snorting of horses proclaimed between cavalry.

Never was conflict of shorter duration ; over
almost before they in the courtyard could
realise its having commenced.  The confused
sounds of the melée lasted barely a minute
when a loud huzza, drowning the hoof-strokes
of the retreating horses, told that victory had
declared itself for one side or the other.  They
who listened were not long in doubt as to
which sent up that triumphant cheer.  Through
the front gate, standing open, burst a mass of
mounted men, some carrying lances couched
for the thrust, others with drawn sabres, many
of their blades dripping blood.  On came they

into the courtyard, still vociferating : " Mueran los tyrannos !" while he at their head soon as showing himself, called out in a commanding voice, " Rendite ?"

By this a change had taken place in the tableau of figures beside the carriage. The Hussars having reined back, had gathered in a ruck around their colonel, irresolute how to act. Equally unresolved he to order them. That cry, " Country and Liberty," had struck terror to his heart; and now seeing those it came from, recognising the three who rode foremost—as in the clear moonlight he could —the blood of the craven ran cold. They were the men he had subjected to insult, direct degradation ; and he need look for no mercy at their hands. With a spark of manhood, even such as despair sometimes inspires, he would have shown fight. Major Ramirez would, and did ; for at the first alarm he had galloped out to the gate and there met death.

Not so Santander, who, although he had taken his sword out of its scabbard, made no attempt to use it, but sat shivering in his saddle as if the weapon was about to drop from his hand.

On the instant after a blade more firmly held, and better wielded, flashed before his eyes ; he who held it, as he sprung his horse up, crying out :

"Carlos Santander ! your hour has come ! Scoundrel ! *This time* I intend killing you."

Even the insulting threat stung him not to resistance. Never shone moonlight on more of a poltroon, the glitter and grandeur of his warlike dress in striking contrast with his cowardly mien.

"Miserable wretch," cried Kearney—for it was he who confronted him—" I don't want to kill you in cold blood. Heaven forbid my doing murder. Defend yourself."

" He defend hisself !" scornfully exclaimed a voice—that of Cris Rock. " He dassen't as much as do that. He hasn't the steel shirt on now."

Yet another voice at this moment made itself heard, as a figure feminine became added to the group. Luisa Valverde it was, who, rushing out of the carriage and across the courtyard, cried out—

" Spare his life, Don Florencio. He's not worthy of your sword."

" You're right thar, young lady," endorsed the Texan, answering for Kearney. " That he ain't—an' bare worth the bit o' lead that's inside o' this ole pistol. For all, I'll make him a present o' 't—thar, dang ye."

The last words were accompanied by a flash and a crack, causing Santander's horse to shy and rear up. When the fore hoofs of the animal returned to the flags, they but missed coming down upon the body of its rider, now lying lifeless along them.

"That's gin him his quieetus, I reckin," observed Rock, as he glanced down at the dead man, whose face upturned had the full moonlight upon it, showing handsome features, that withal were forbidding in life, but now more so in the ghastly pallor of death.

No one stayed to gaze upon them, least of all the Texan ; who had yet another life to take, as he deemed in the strict execution duty and satisfaction of justice. For it too was forfeit by the basest betrayal. The soldiers were out of their saddles now, prisoners all ; having surrendered without striking a blow. But crouching away in a shadowy corner was that thing of deformity, who, from his diminutive size might well

have escaped observation. He did not, however. The Texan had his eyes on him all
the while, having caught a glimpse of him
as they were riding in at the gate. And in
those eyes now gleamed the light of a
vengeance not to be allayed save by a life
sacrificed. If Santander on seeing Kearney
believed his hour was come, so did the dwarf
as he saw Cris Rock striding towards him.
Caught by the collar, and dragged out into
the light he knew death was near now.

In vain his protestations and piteous
appeals. Spite of all, he had to die. And
a death so unlike that usually meted out to
criminals, as he himself to the commonality
of men. No weapon was employed in putting
an end to him ; neither gun nor pistol, sword
nor knife. Letting go hold of his collar,
the Texan grasped him around the ankles,
and with a brandish raising him aloft, brought

his head down upon the pavement. There was a crash as the breaking of a cocoa-nut shell by a hammer; and when Rock let go, the mass of mis-shapen humanity dropped in a dollop upon the flags, arms and legs limp and motionless, in the last not even the power left for a spasmodic kick.

"Ye know, Cap.," said the Texan, justifying himself to Kearney, "I'd be the last man to do a cruel thing. But to rid the world o' sech varmint as them, 'cording to my way o' thinking, air the purest hewmanity."

A doctrine which the young Irishman was not disposed to dispute just at that time, being otherwise and better occupied, holding soft hands in his, words exchanging with sweet lips, not unaccompanied by kisses. Near at hand Don Ruperto was doing the same, his *vis-a-vis* being the Condesa.

But these moments of bliss were brief—had

need be. The raid of the Free Lances down to San Augustin was a thing of risk, only to have been attempted by lovers who believed their loved ones were in deadly danger. In another hour or less, the Hussars who had escaped would report themselves at San Angel and Chapultepec—then there would be a rush of thousands in the direction of Tlalpam.

So there was in reality—soldiers of all arms, "horse, foot, and dragoons". But on arrival there they found the house of Don Ignacio Valverde untenanted; even the domestics had gone out of it; the carriage, too, which has played such an important part in our tale, along with the noble frisones. The horses had not been taken out of it, nor any change made in the company it carried off. Only in the driver, the direction, and cortege. José again held the reins, heading his horses up the mountain road, instead of towards

Mexico; while in place of Colonel Santander's Hussars, the Free Lances of Captain Ruperto Rivas now formed a more friendly escort.

# CHAPTER LXI.

## CONCLUSION.

ABOUT a month after in San Augustin, a small two-masted vessel—a goleta —might have been observed standing on tacks off the coast of Oaxaca, as if working against the land wind to make to the mouth of Rio Tecoyama—a stream which runs into the Pacific near the south-western corner of that State. Only sharp eyes could have seen the schooner; for it was

3—14

night, and the night was a very dark one. There were eyes sharply on the look-out for her, however, anxiously scanning the horizon to leeward, some of them through glasses. On an elevated spot among the mangroves, by the river's mouth, a party was assembled, in all, about a score individuals. They were mostly men, though not exclusively; three female figures being distinguishable, as forming part of the group. Two of them had the air, and wore the dress, of ladies, somewhat torn and travel-stained; the third was in the guise of a maid-servant attending them. They were the Condesa Almonté, the Don Luisa Valverde, and her ever faithful Pepita.

Among the men were six, with whom the reader has acquaintance. Don Ignacio, Kearney, Rock, Rivas, José, and he who had been major-domo in the old monastery, baptismally named Gregorio. Most of the others, undescribed, had also spent some time in the establishment with the monks while playing the part of Free Lances. They were, in fact, a remnant of the band—now broken up and dispersed.

But why! When last seen it looked as though their day of triumph had come, or was at all events near. So would it have been but for a betrayal, through which the *pronunciamento* had miscarried, or rather did not come off. The Dictator, well informed about it—further warned by what occurred at San Augustin—had poured troops over the Sierras into Oaxaca in force sufficient to awe the leaders of the intended insurrection. It was but by the breadth of a hair that his late Cabinet Minister, and those who accompanied him, were able to escape to the sequestered spot where we find them, on the shore of the South Sea. To Alvarez, chief of the Pintos, or "spotted Indians," were they indebted for safe conduct thither; he himself having adroitly kept clear of all compromise consequent on that grito unraised. Furthermore, he had promised to provide them with a vessel in which they might escape out of the country; and it was for this they were now on the look-out.

When Ruperto Rivas, gazing through that same telescope he had given Florence Kearney to make survey of the valley of Mexico, cried out, " La goleta ! " every eye around him brightened, every heart beat joyously.

Still more rejoiced were they when, after an hour's tacking against the land breeze, the goleta got inside the estuary of the stream, and working up, brought to by the edge of the mangroves.

Unencumbered with heavy baggage, they were all soon aboard, and in three days after debarked at the port of Panama. Thence crossing the Isthmus to Chagres, another sea-going craft carried them on to the city, where they need no longer live in fear of Mexico's despot.

Back to his old quarters in New Orleans had Don Ignacio repaired; again under the ban of proscription, his estates sequestrated as before. So, too, those of the Condésa Almonté.

But not for all time, believed they. They lived in hope of a restoration.

Nor were they disappointed; for it came. The *pronunciamento* delayed was at length proclaimed, and carried to a successful issue. Once again throughout the land of Anahuac had arisen a " grito," its battle cry " Patria y Libertad ! " so earnestly and loudly shouted as to drive the Dictator from his mock throne ; sending him, as several times before, to seek safety in a foreign land.

Nor were the " Free Lances " unrepresented in this revolutionary struggle ; instead, they played an important part in it. Ere it broke out, they who had fled the country re-entered it over the Texan border, and rejoining their brethren became once more ranged under the leadership of Captain Ruperto Rivas, with Florence Kearney as his lieutenant, and Cris Rock a sort of attaché to the band, but a valuable adjunct to its fighting force.

\* \* \* \* \* \* \* \*

Swords returned to their scabbards, bugles no longer sounding war signals, it remains but to speak of an episode of more peaceful and pleasanter nature, which occurred at a later period, and not so very long after. The place was inside the Grand Cathedral of Mexico, at whose altar, surrounded by a throng of the land's elite, bells ringing, and organ music vibrating on the air, stood three couples, waiting to be wedded.

And wedded they were; Don Ruperto Rivas to the Condesa Almonté, Florence Kearney to the Dona Luisa Valverde, and— José to Pepita.

Happy they, and happy also one who was but a witness of the ceremony, having a better view of it than most of the spectators, from being the head and shoulders taller than any. Need we say this towering personage was the big Tejano? Cris looked on delightedly, proud of his comrade and protege, with the beautiful bride he had won and was wedding. For all it failed to shake his own faith in single blessedness. In his eyes there was no bride so beautiful as the " Land of the Lone Star," no wife so dear as its wild "purairas". And to them after a time he returned; oft around the camp-fire entertaining his companions of the chase with an account of his adventures in the Mexican valley—how he had there figured in the various roles of jail-bird, scavenger, friar, and last of all as one of the FREE LANCES.

THE END.